CONTENTS

5 A SUPER START!

23 SUPER SEA CREATURES

25 NARWHAL, YOU'RE A SUPERSTAR!

39 SUPER WAFFLE AND STRAWBERRY SIDEKICK!

43 SUPER NARWHAL VS BLUE JELLY
A.K.A. THE SUPER SUPERPOWER!

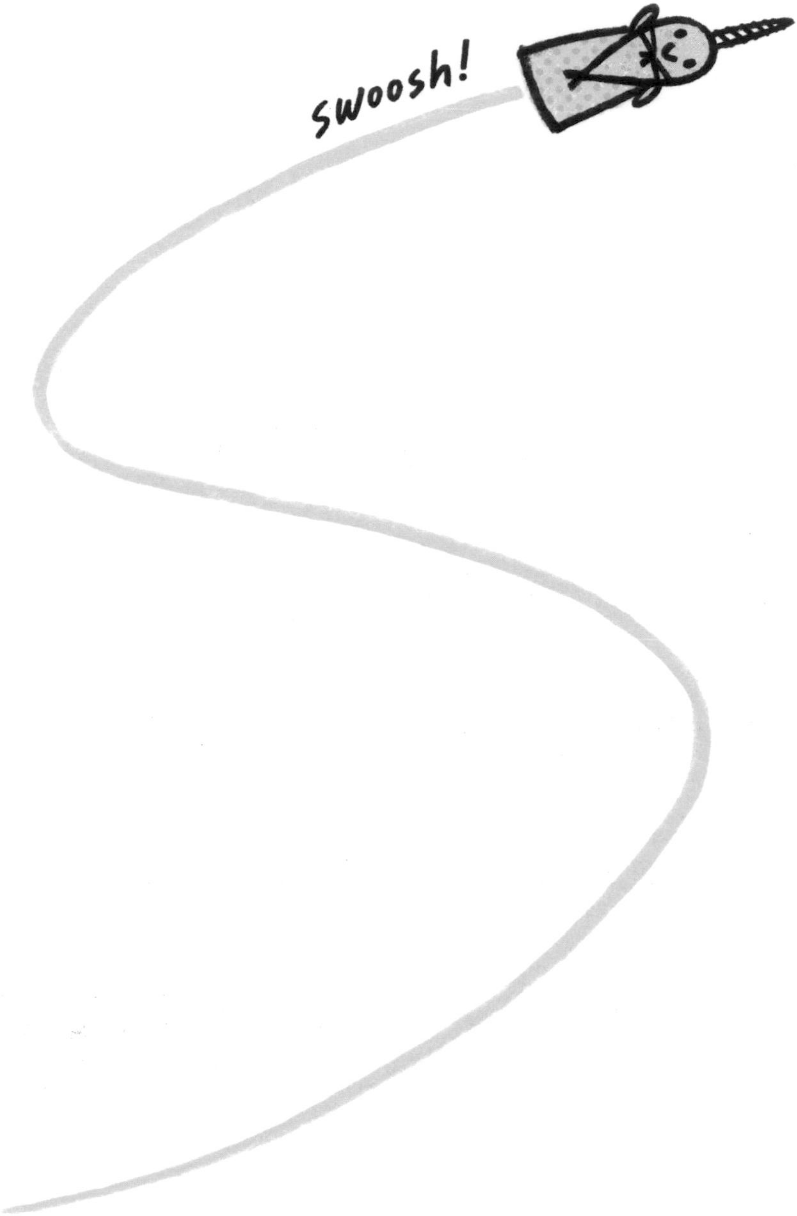
swoosh!

A SUPER START!

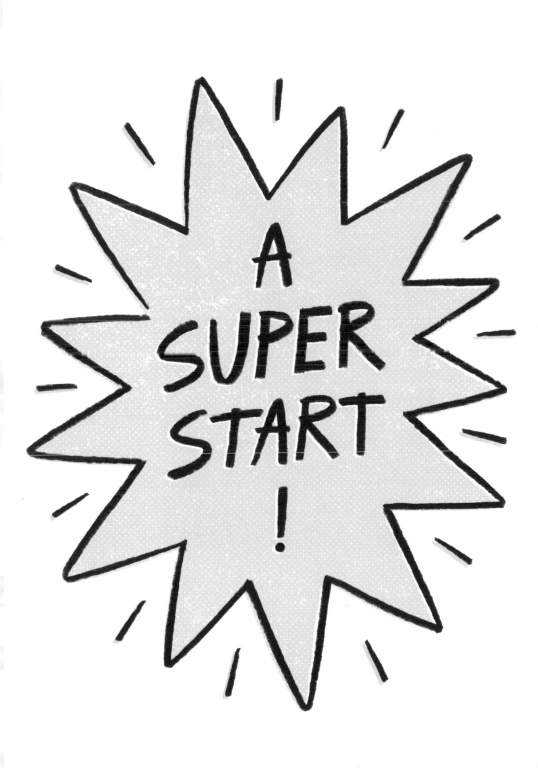

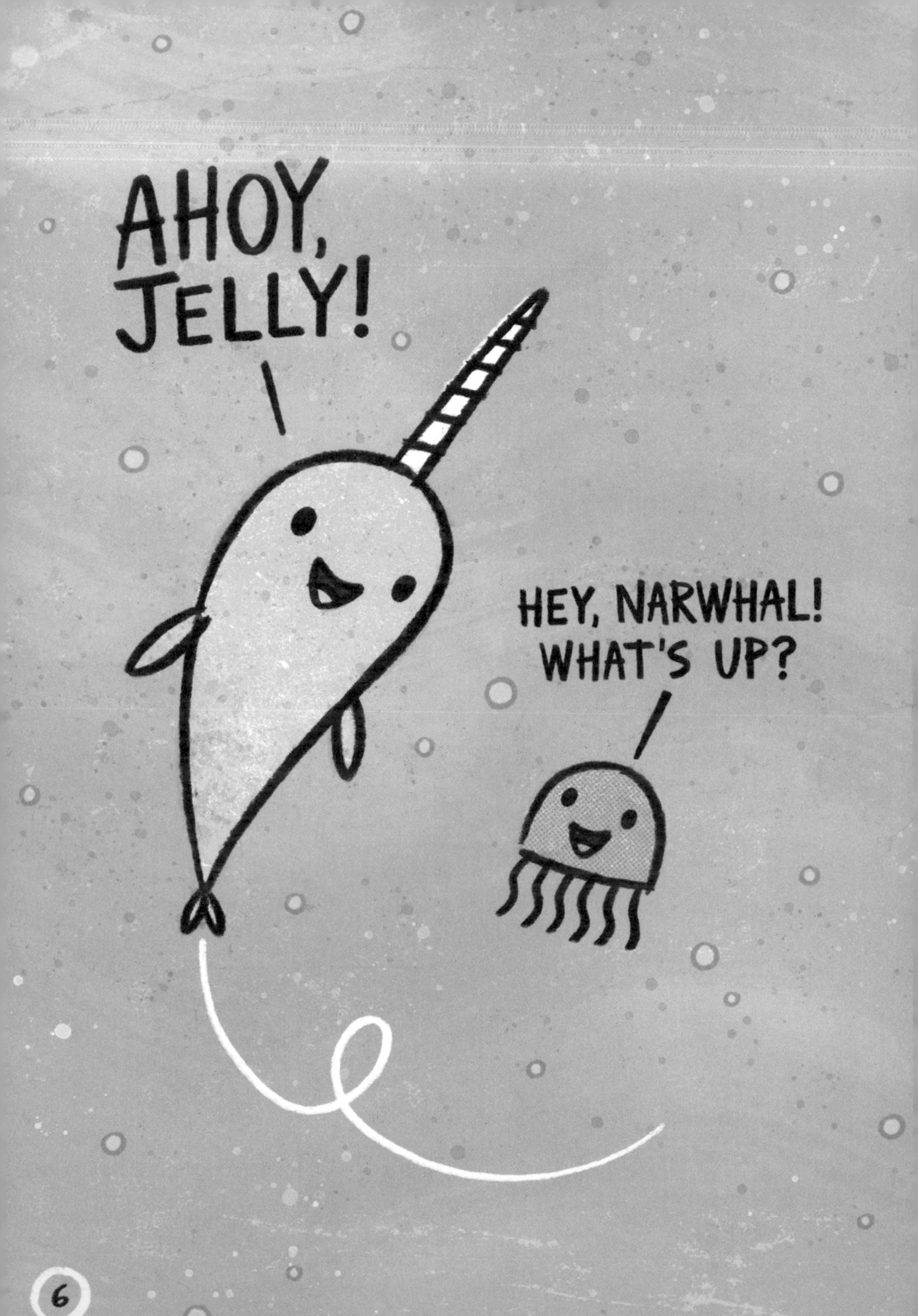
AHOY, JELLY!
HEY, NARWHAL! WHAT'S UP?

SUPER NARWHAL AND JELLY JOLT

BEN CLANTON

Farshore

FOR THEO!
MY SUPER SON!

Farshore

FIRST PUBLISHED IN CANADA 2017 BY TUNDRA BOOKS

FIRST PUBLISHED IN GREAT BRITAIN IN 2019 BY FARSHORE

PUBLISHED BY ARRANGEMENT WITH TUNDRA BOOKS,
AN IMPRINT OF PENGUIN RANDOM HOUSE CANADA YOUNG READERS,
A PENGUIN RANDOM HOUSE COMPANY

AN IMPRINT OF HARPERCOLLINS*PUBLISHERS*
1 LONDON BRIDGE STREET, LONDON SE1 9GF

FARSHORE.CO.UK

HARPERCOLLINS*PUBLISHERS*
1ST FLOOR, WATERMARQUE BUILDING,
RINGSEND ROAD, DUBLIN 4, IRELAND

TEXT AND ILLUSTRATIONS COPYRIGHT © 2017 BEN CLANTON

ISBN 978 1 4052 9531 4
PRINTED IN ITALY
5

A CIP CATALOGUE RECORD FOR THIS TITLE IS AVAILABLE FROM THE BRITISH LIBRARY

MIX
Paper from
responsible sources
FSC™ C007454

FSC
www.fsc.org

This book is produced from independently certified FSC™ paper
to ensure responsible forest management.

For more information visit: www.harpercollins.co.uk/green

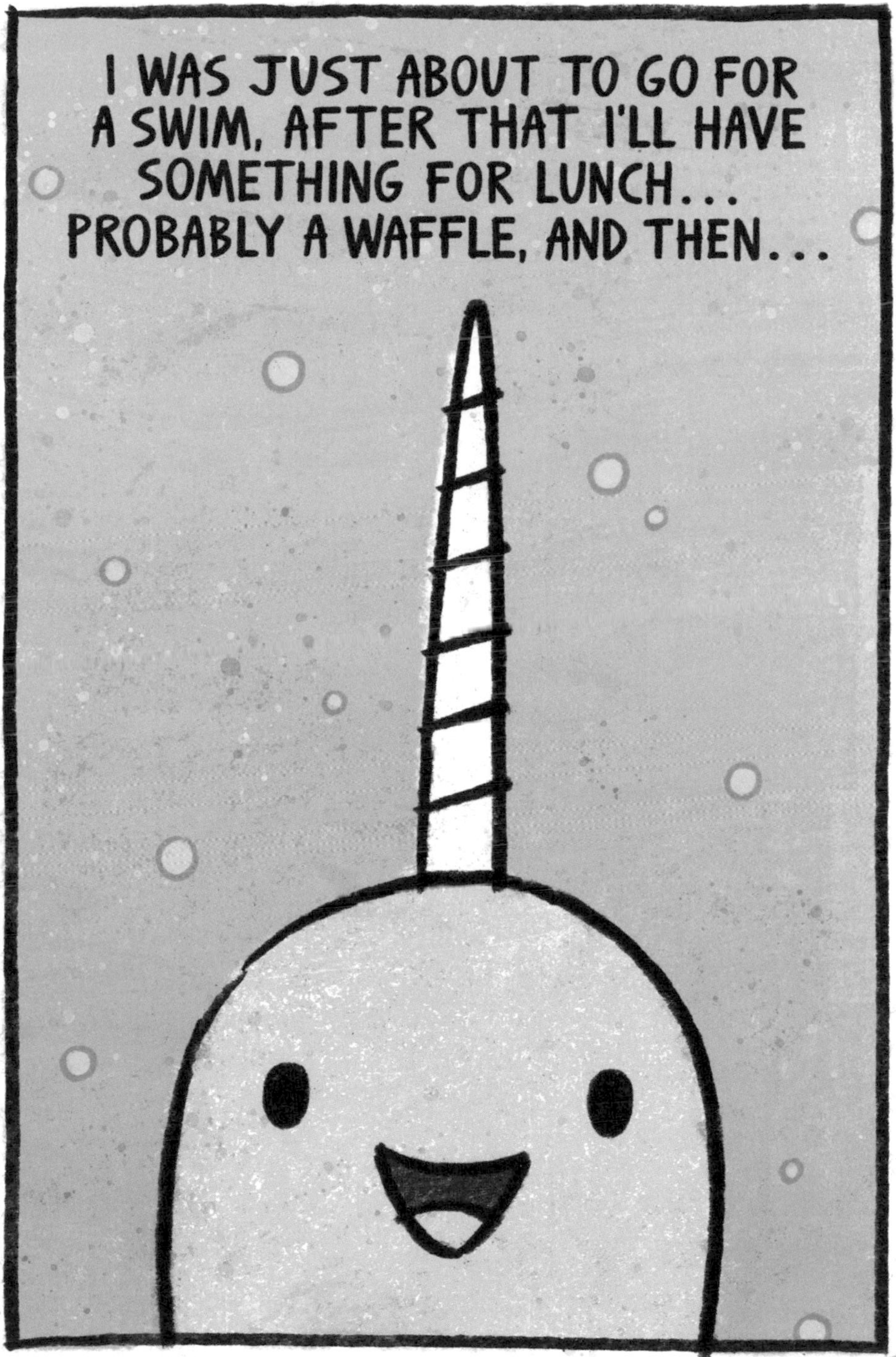
I WAS JUST ABOUT TO GO FOR A SWIM, AFTER THAT I'LL HAVE SOMETHING FOR LUNCH... PROBABLY A WAFFLE, AND THEN...

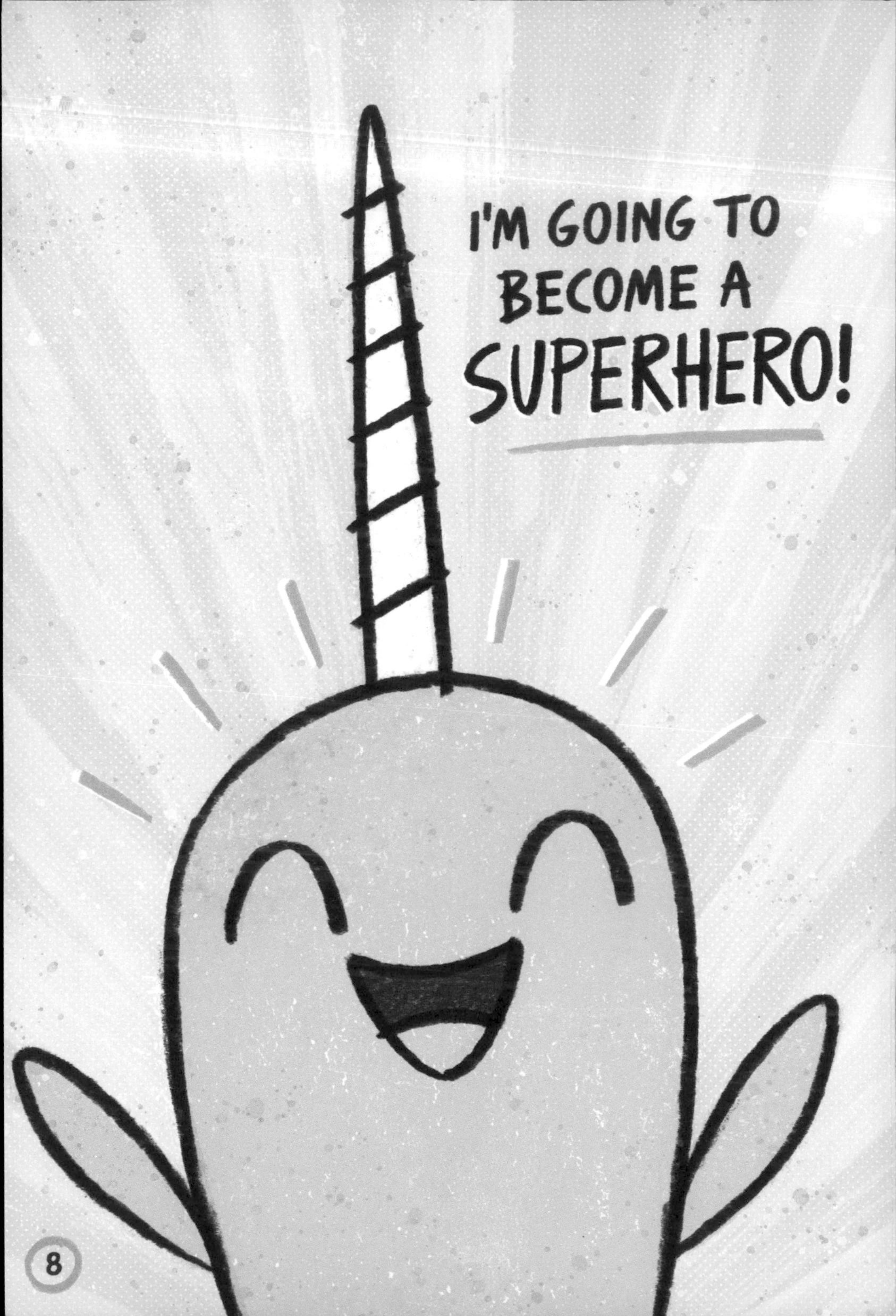
I'M GOING TO BECOME A SUPERHERO!

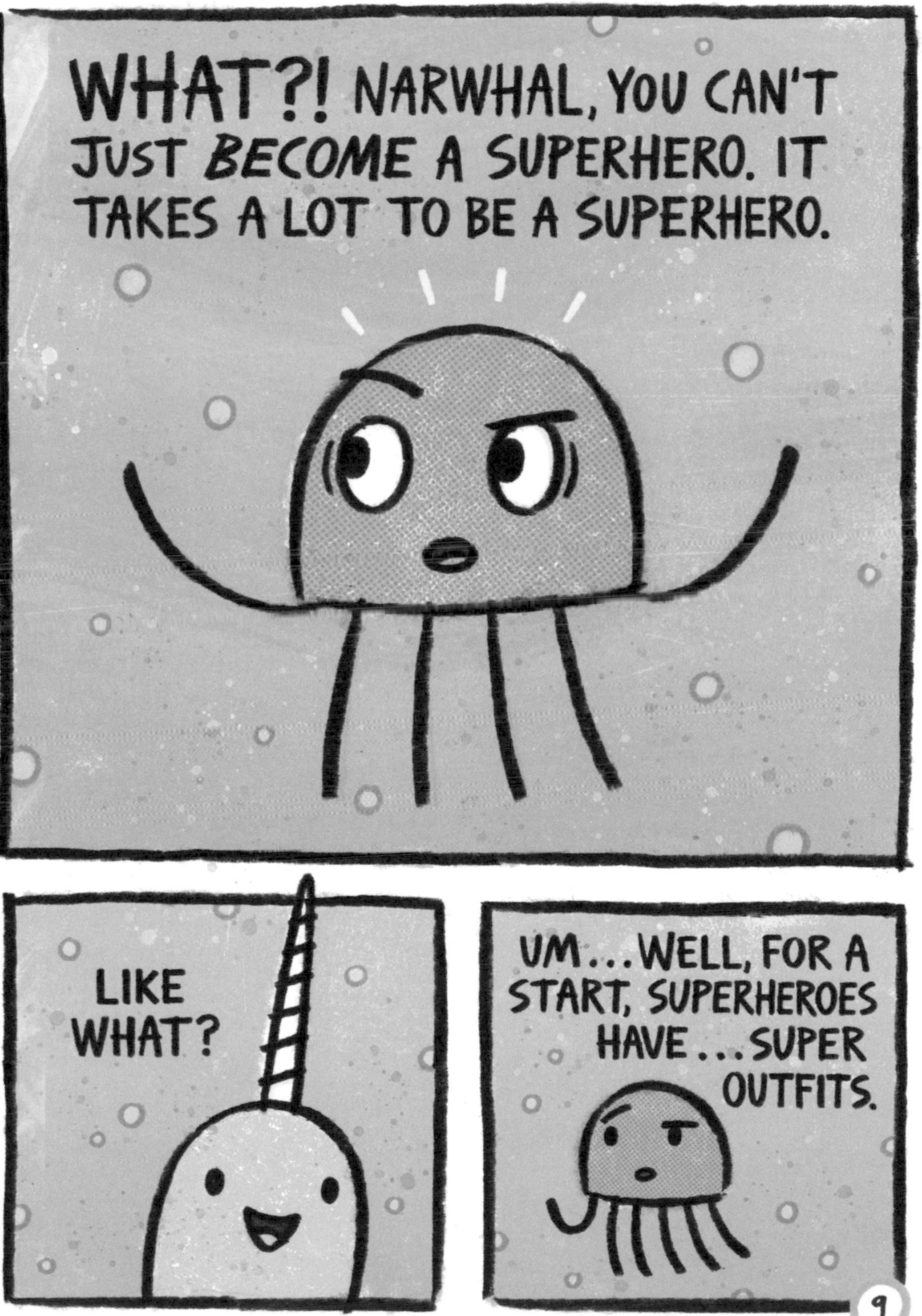
WHAT?! NARWHAL, YOU CAN'T JUST *BECOME* A SUPERHERO. IT TAKES A LOT TO BE A SUPERHERO.
LIKE WHAT?
UM...WELL, FOR A START, SUPERHEROES HAVE...SUPER OUTFITS.

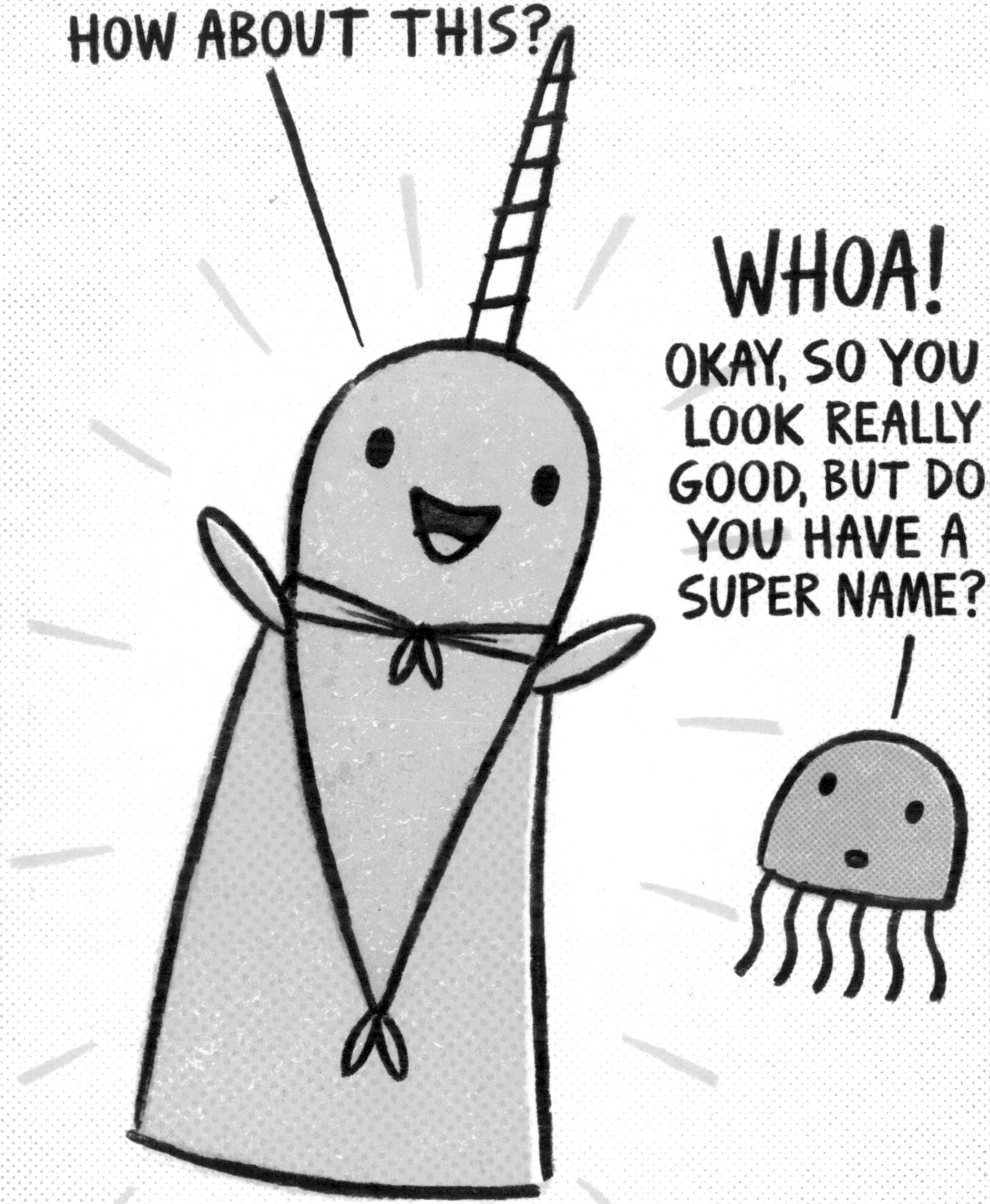
HOW ABOUT THIS?
WHOA!
OKAY, SO YOU LOOK REALLY GOOD, BUT DO YOU HAVE A SUPER NAME?

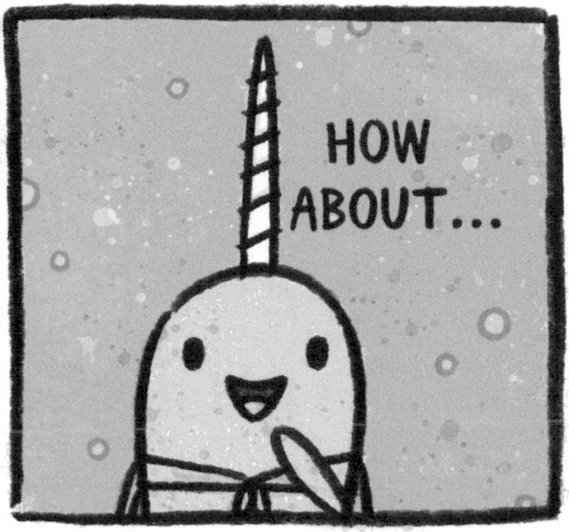
HOW ABOUT...

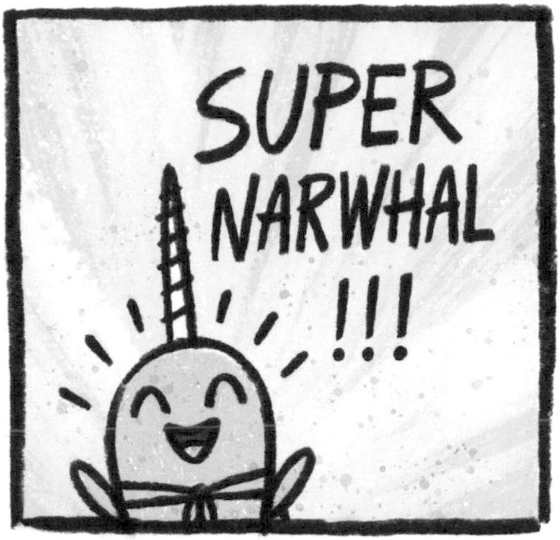
SUPER NARWHAL !!!

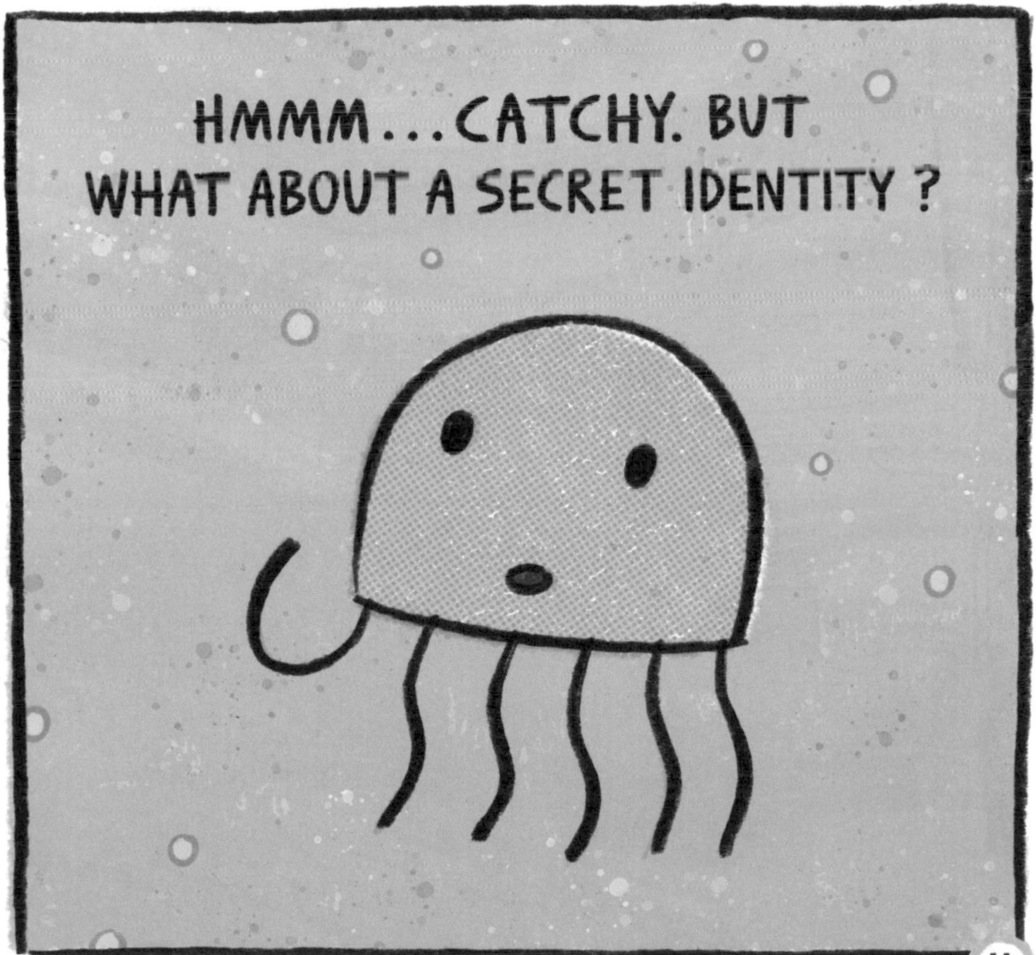
HMMM...CATCHY. BUT WHAT ABOUT A SECRET IDENTITY ?

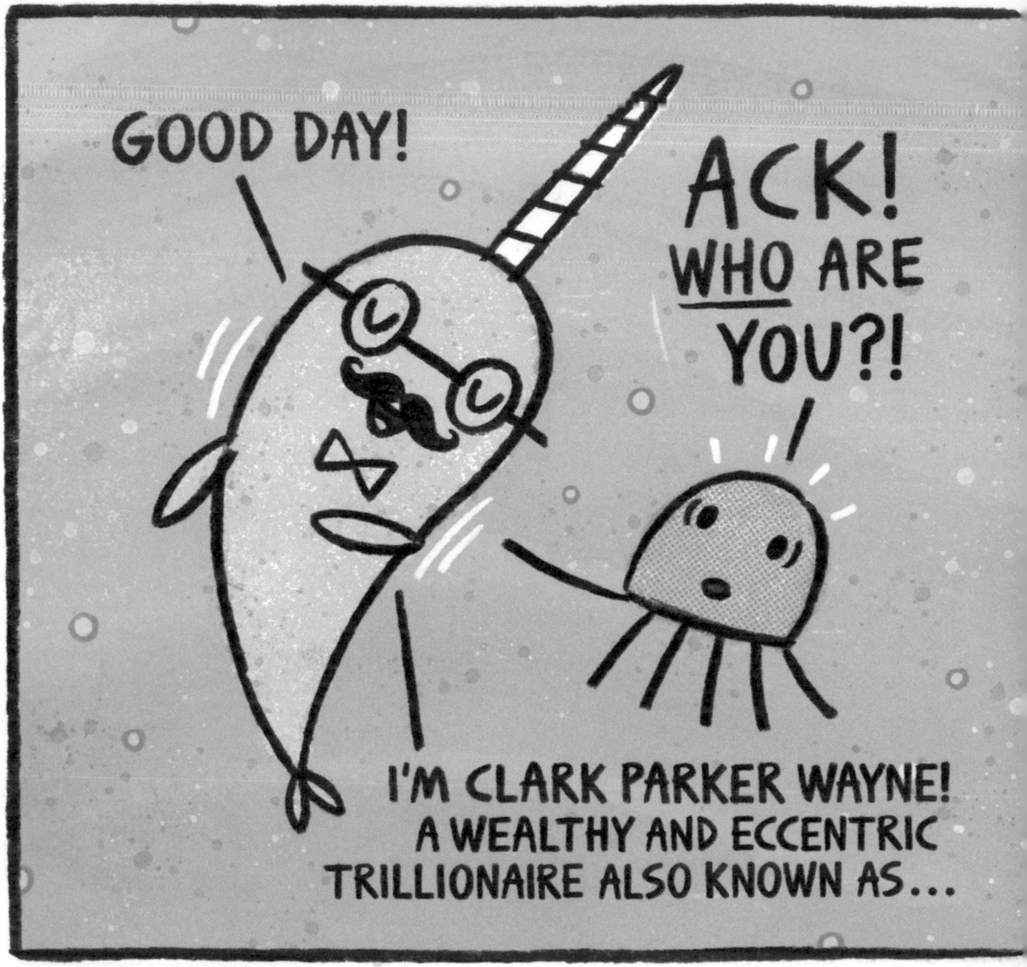
GOOD DAY!
ACK! WHO ARE YOU?!
I'M CLARK PARKER WAYNE! A WEALTHY AND ECCENTRIC TRILLIONAIRE ALSO KNOWN AS...

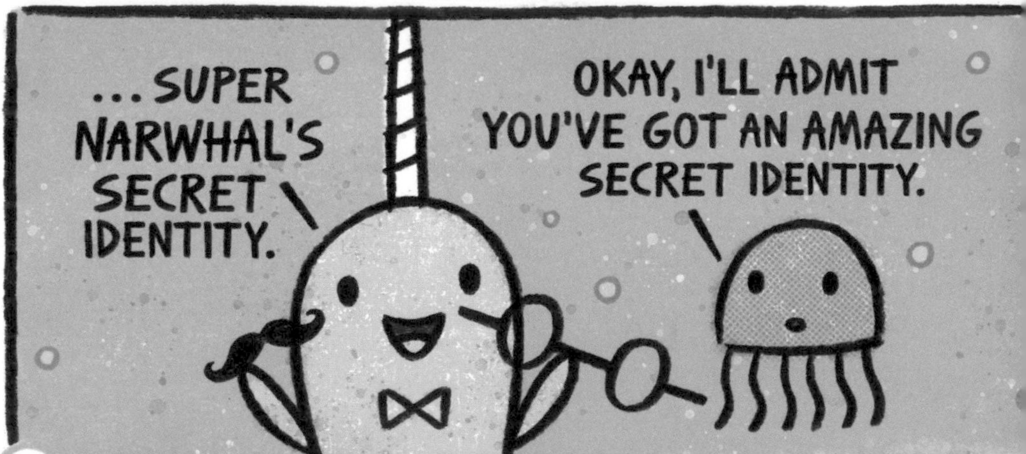
...SUPER NARWHAL'S SECRET IDENTITY.
OKAY, I'LL ADMIT YOU'VE GOT AN AMAZING SECRET IDENTITY.

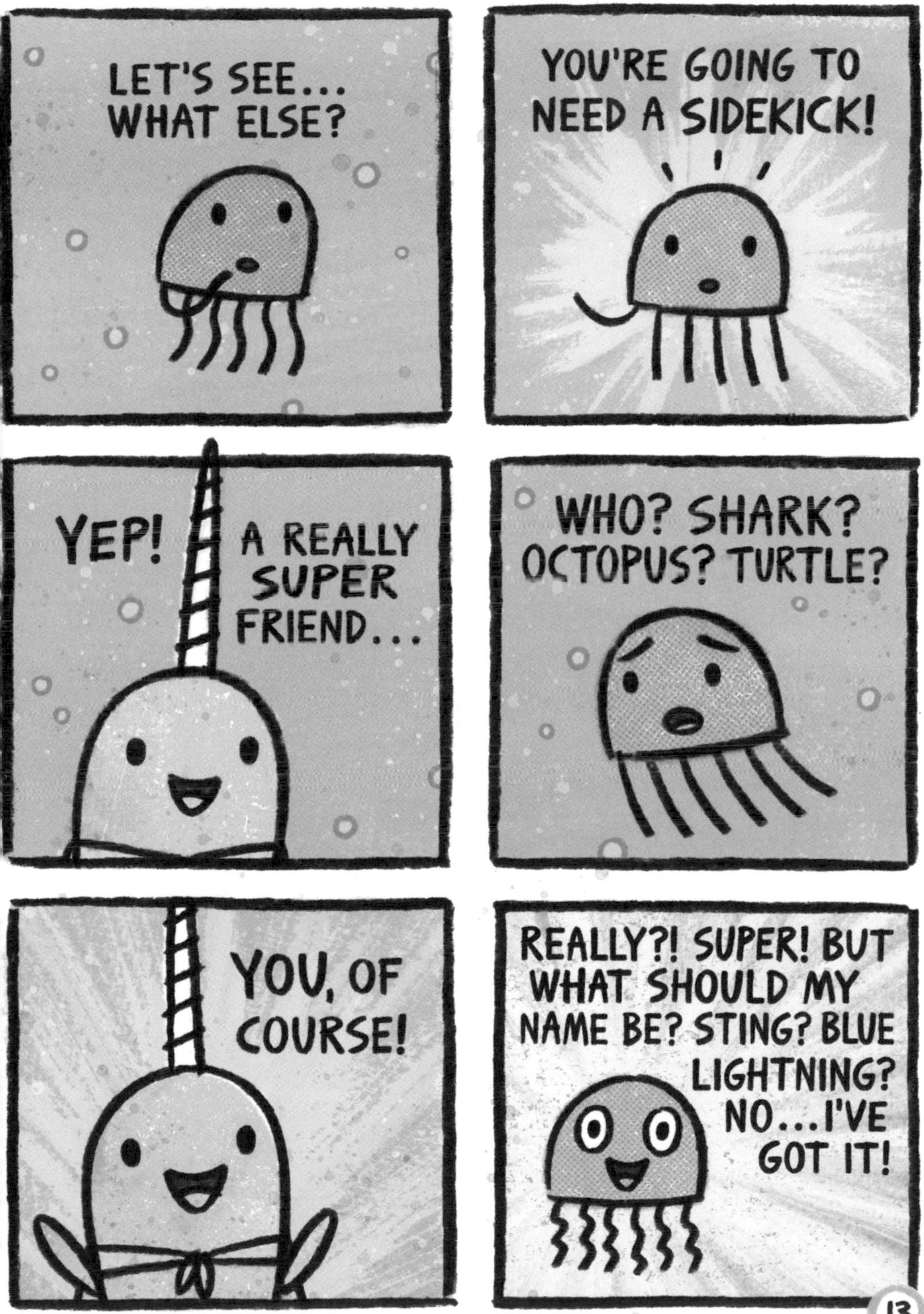
LET'S SEE... WHAT ELSE?
YOU'RE GOING TO NEED A SIDEKICK!
YEP!
A REALLY SUPER FRIEND...
WHO? SHARK? OCTOPUS? TURTLE?
YOU, OF COURSE!
REALLY?! SUPER! BUT WHAT SHOULD MY NAME BE? STING? BLUE LIGHTNING? NO...I'VE GOT IT!

JELLY JOLT THE SUPER SIDEKICK!

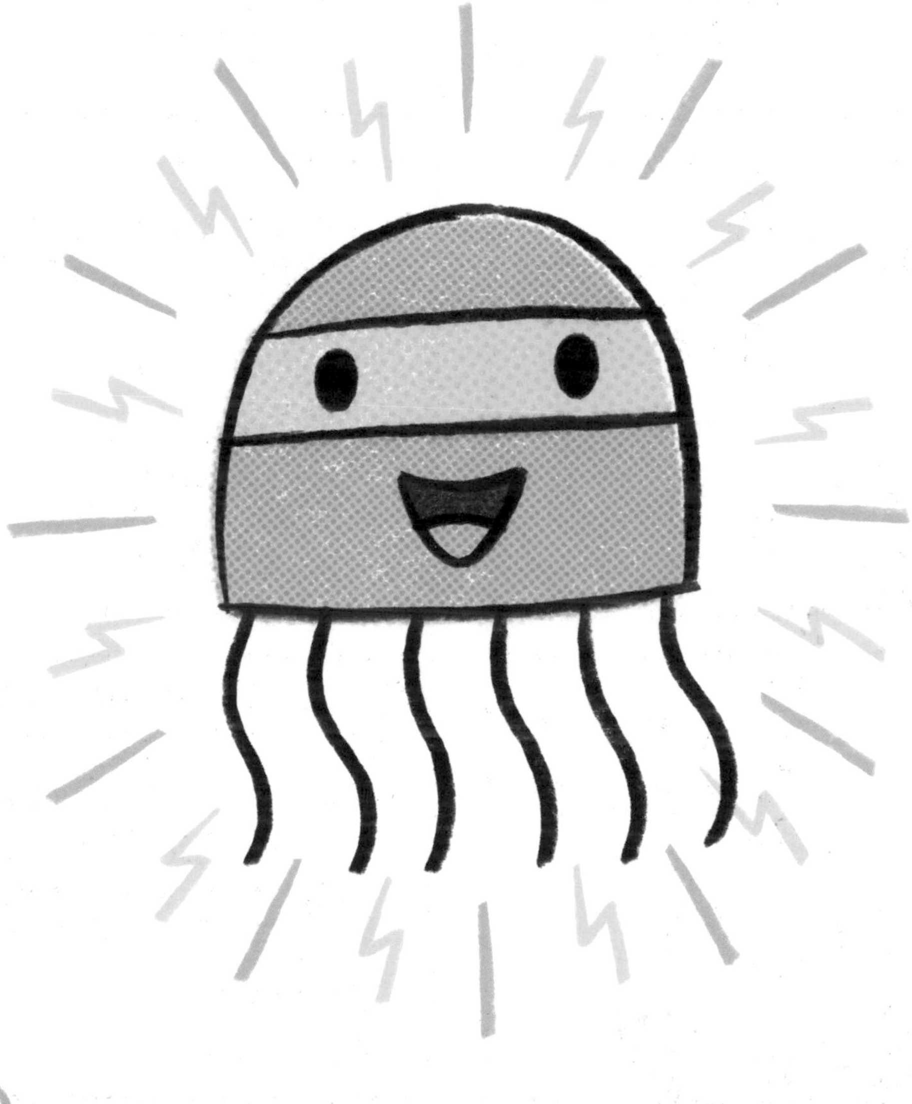

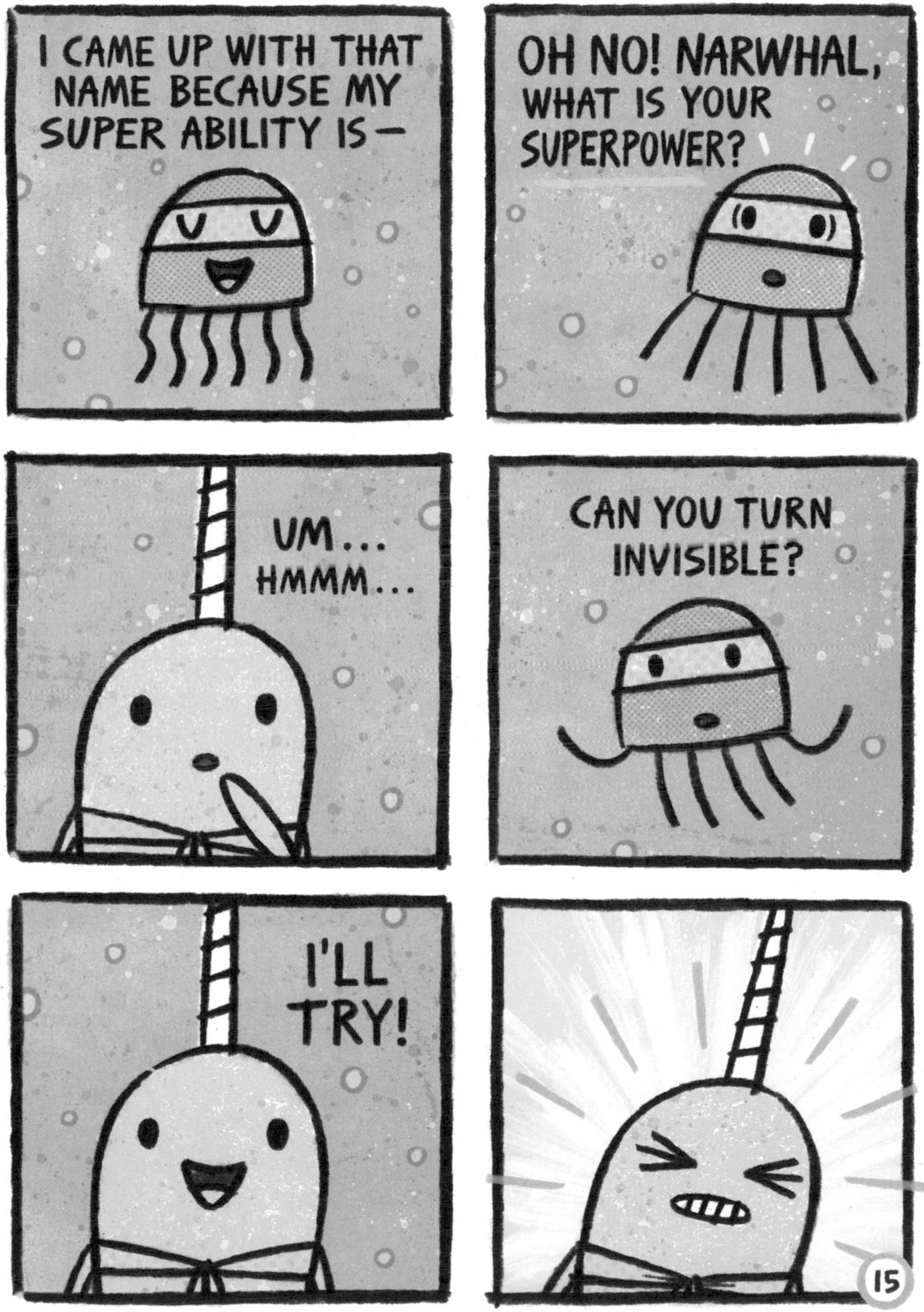
I CAME UP WITH THAT NAME BECAUSE MY SUPER ABILITY IS—
OH NO! NARWHAL, WHAT IS YOUR SUPERPOWER?
UM... HMMM...
CAN YOU TURN INVISIBLE?
I'LL TRY!

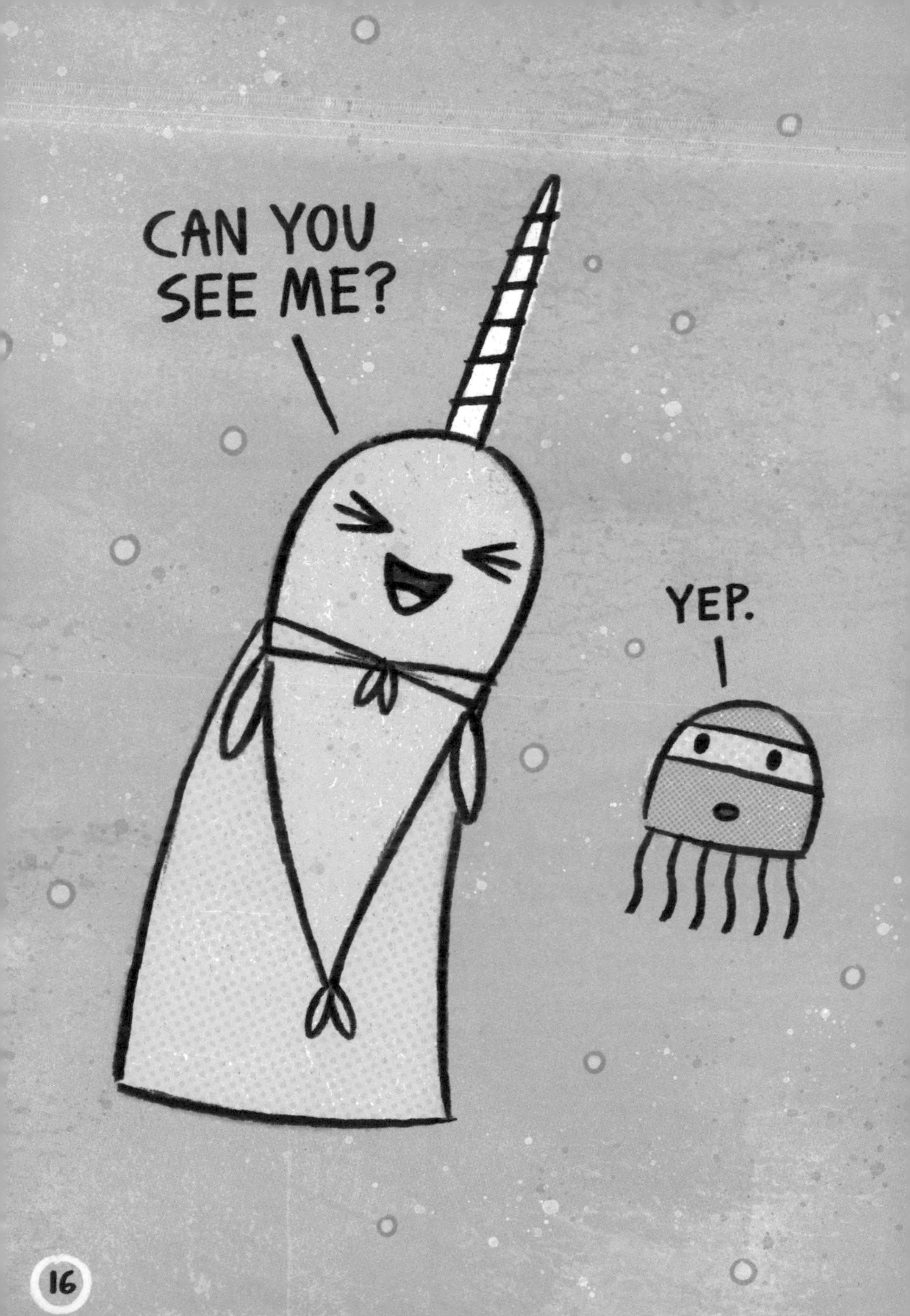
CAN YOU SEE ME?
YEP.

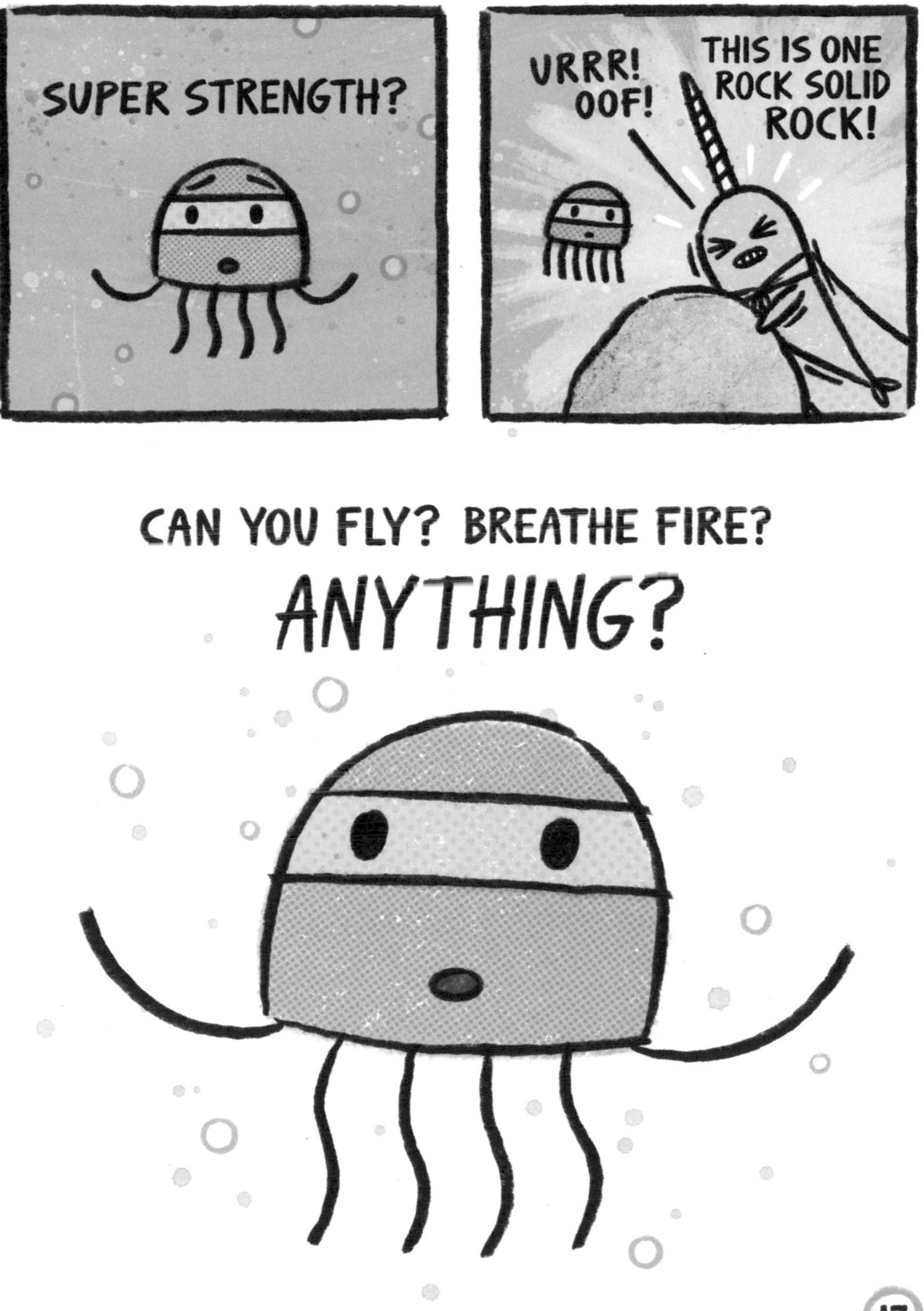
SUPER STRENGTH?
URRR! OOF!
THIS IS ONE ROCK SOLID ROCK!
CAN YOU FLY? BREATHE FIRE?
ANYTHING?

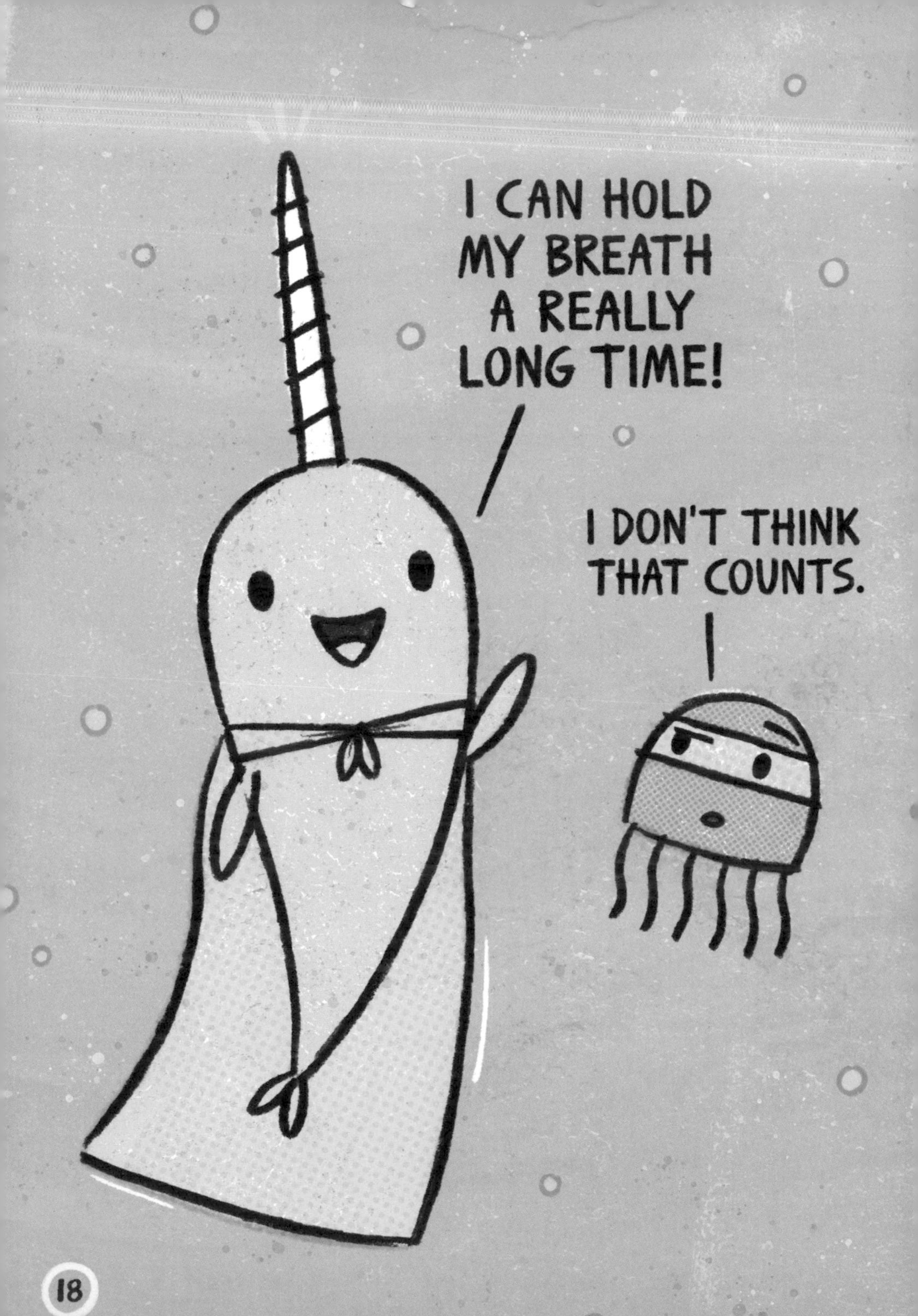
I CAN HOLD MY BREATH A REALLY LONG TIME!
I DON'T THINK THAT COUNTS.

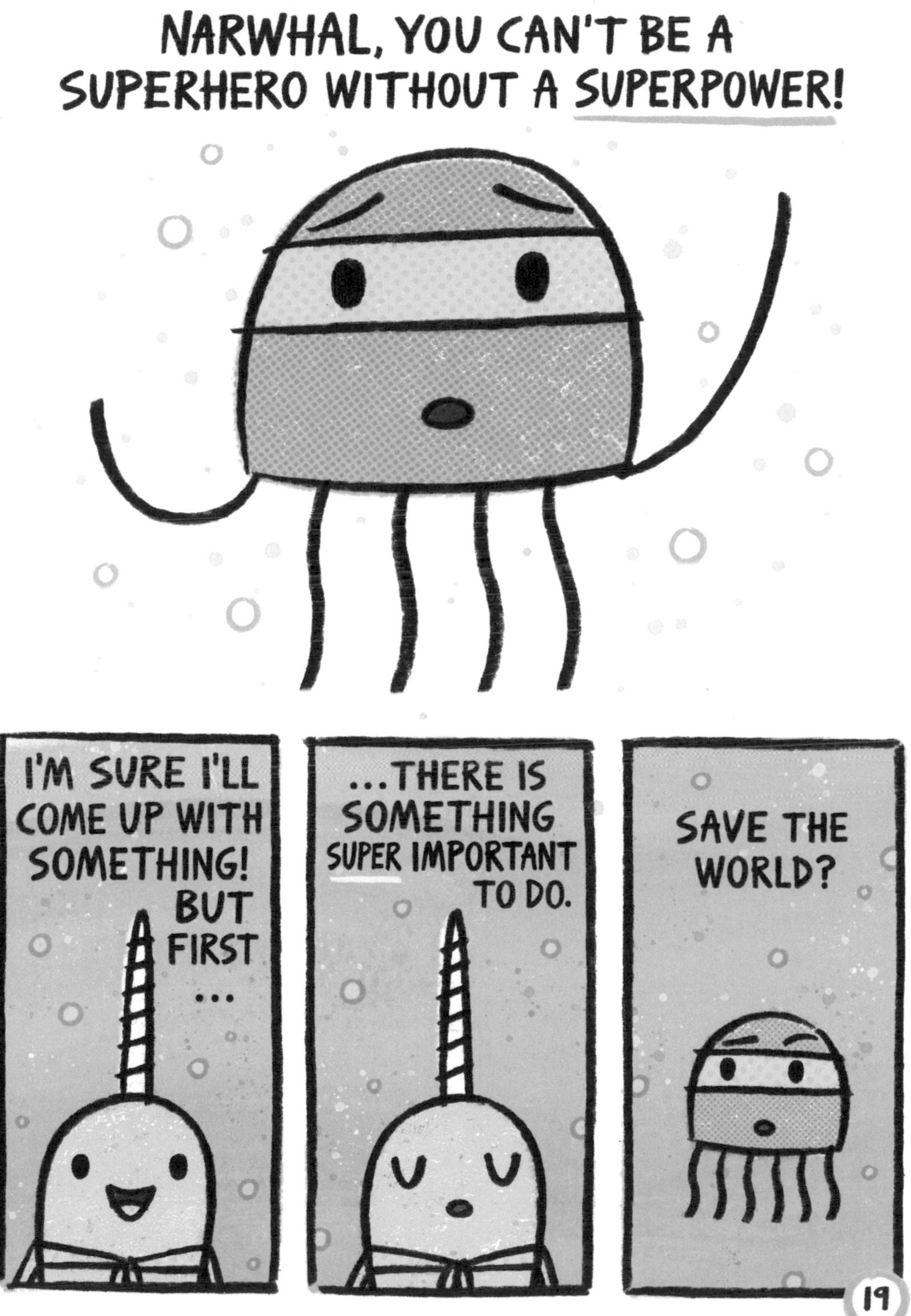
NARWHAL, YOU CAN'T BE A SUPERHERO WITHOUT A SUPERPOWER!
I'M SURE I'LL COME UP WITH SOMETHING! BUT FIRST ...
...THERE IS SOMETHING SUPER IMPORTANT TO DO.
SAVE THE WORLD?

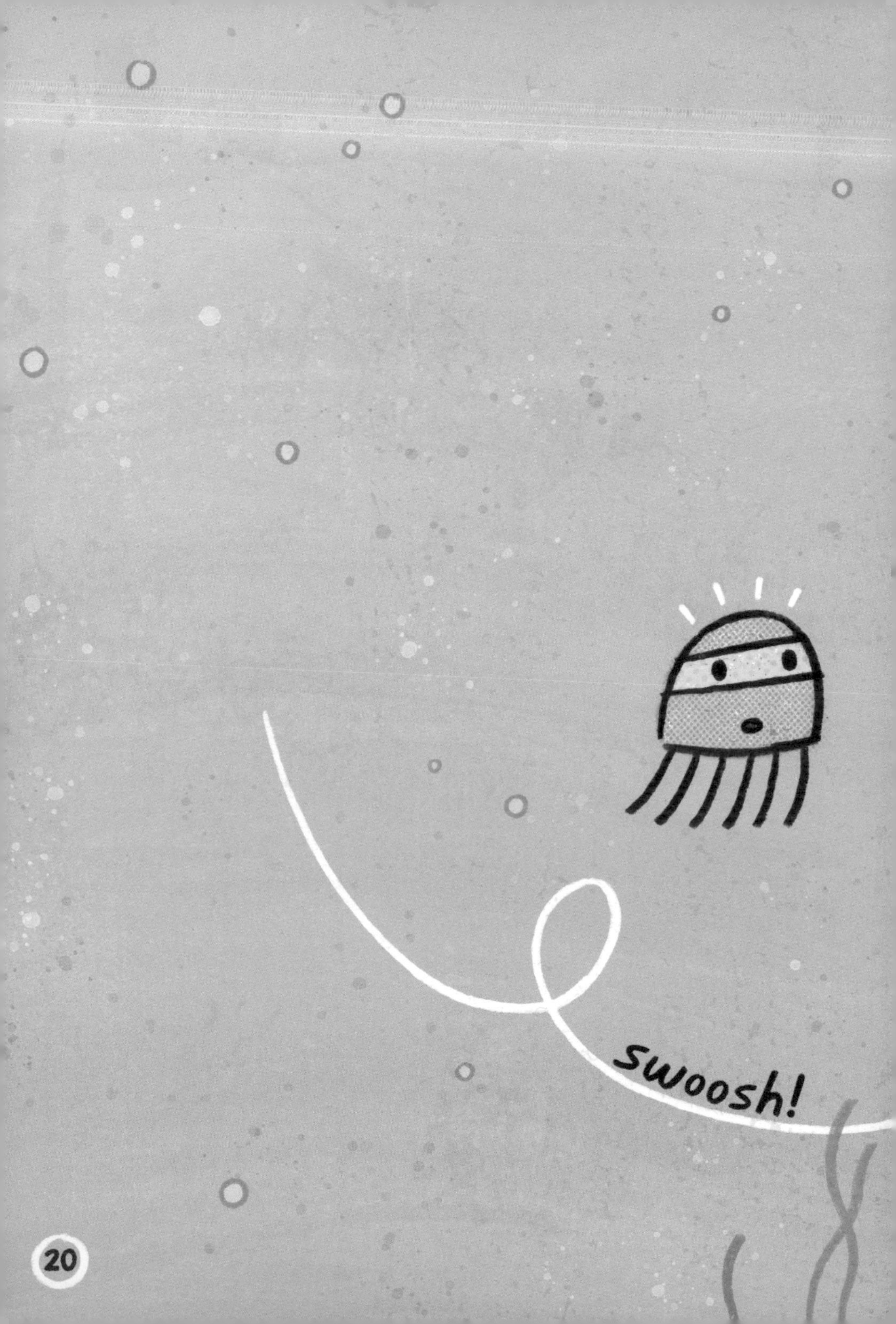
swoosh!

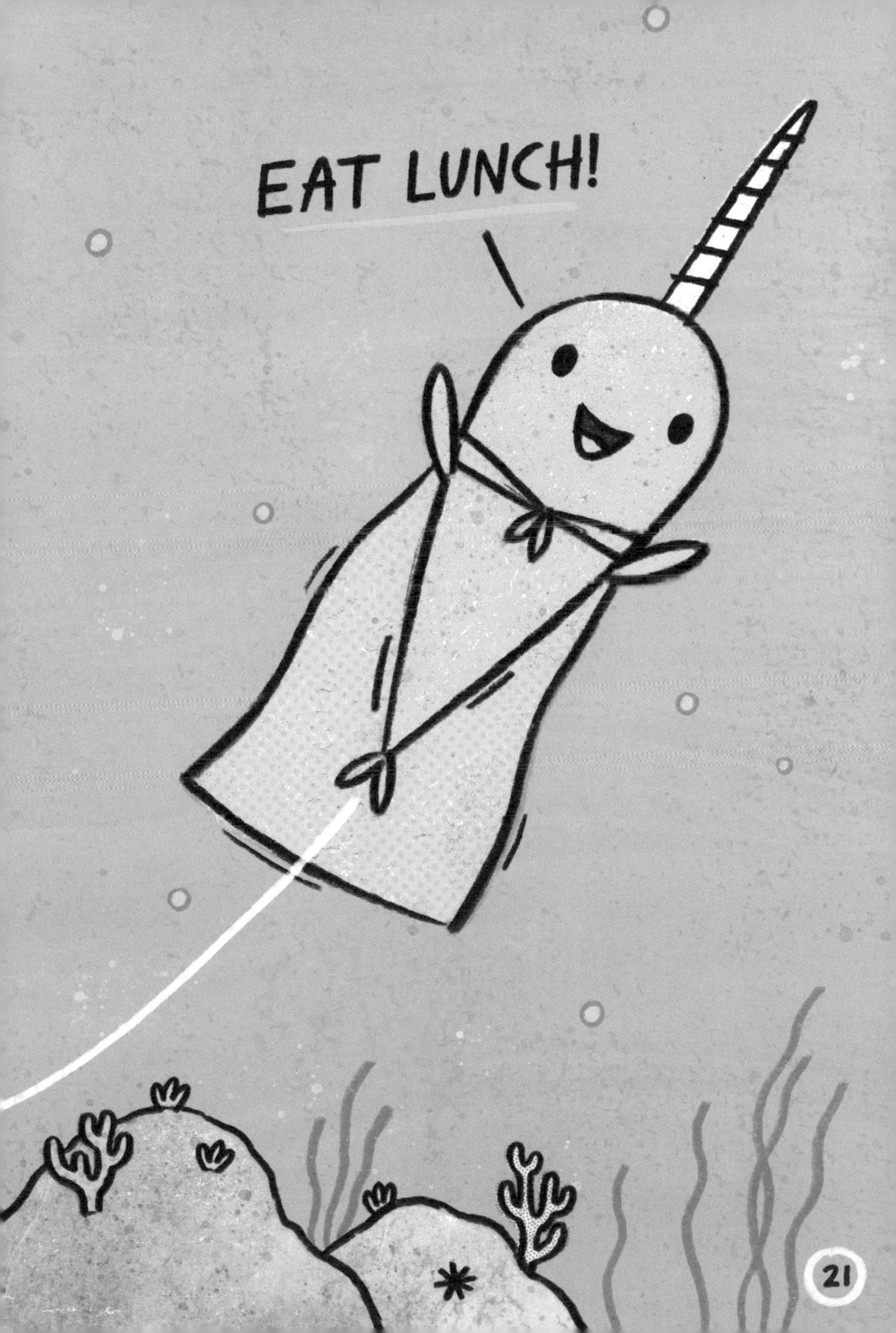
EAT LUNCH!

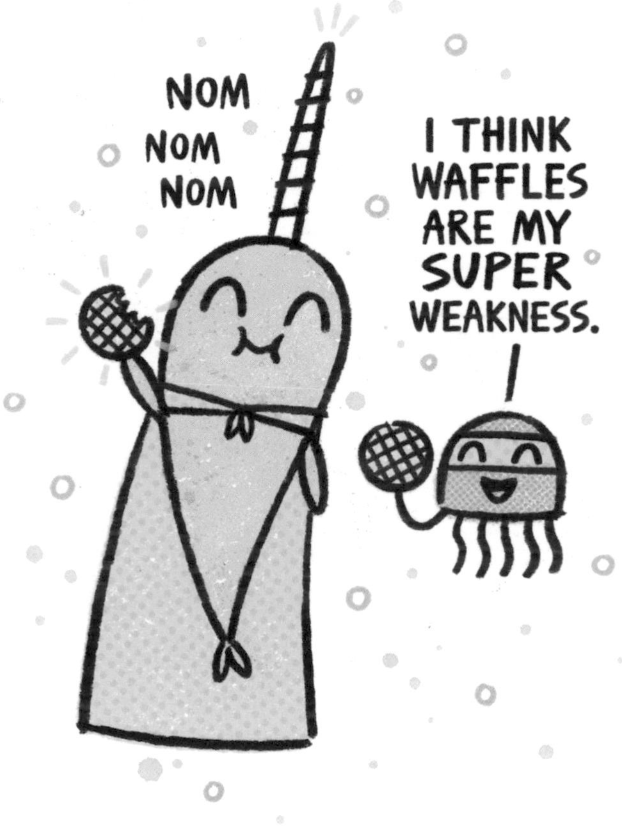
NOM
NOM
NOM
I THINK WAFFLES ARE MY SUPER WEAKNESS.

SUPER SEA CREATURES

REAL SEA CREATURES WITH REAL SUPER-AWESOME ABILITIES

THE MIMIC OCTOPUS CAN CHANGE ITS COLOUR, SHAPE AND MOVEMENTS TO LOOK LIKE OTHER SEA LIFE SUCH AS SNAKES, LIONFISH, STINGRAYS AND JELLYFISH.

STOP COPYING ME!

STOP COPYING ME!

DOLPHINS SLEEP WITH ONLY HALF OF THEIR BRAIN AND WITH ONE EYE OPEN TO WATCH FOR THREATS.

DOLPHINS CAN ALSO 'SEE' INSIDE MANY ANIMALS BY USING SOUND WAVES.

I SEE YOU HAD A WAFFLE FOR LUNCH!

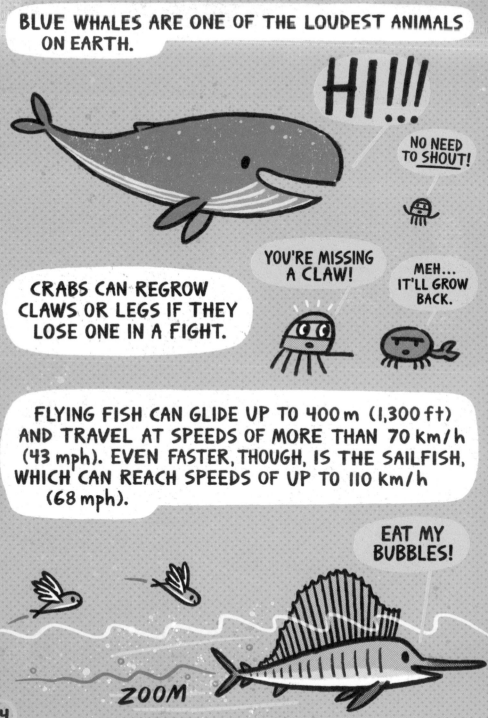

BLUE WHALES ARE ONE OF THE LOUDEST ANIMALS ON EARTH.

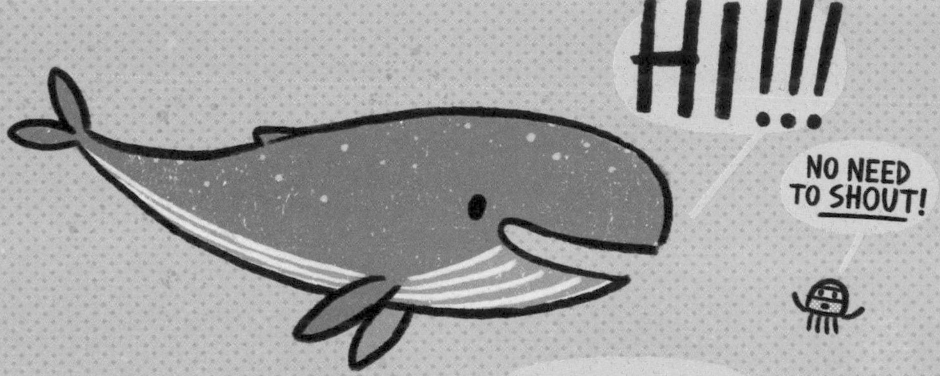
HI!!!...
NO NEED TO SHOUT!

CRABS CAN REGROW CLAWS OR LEGS IF THEY LOSE ONE IN A FIGHT.

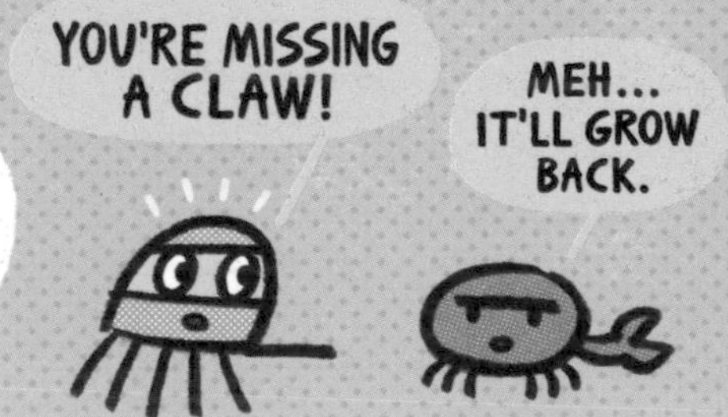
YOU'RE MISSING A CLAW!
MEH... IT'LL GROW BACK.

FLYING FISH CAN GLIDE UP TO 400 m (1,300 ft) AND TRAVEL AT SPEEDS OF MORE THAN 70 km/h (43 mph). EVEN FASTER, THOUGH, IS THE SAILFISH, WHICH CAN REACH SPEEDS OF UP TO 110 km/h (68 mph).

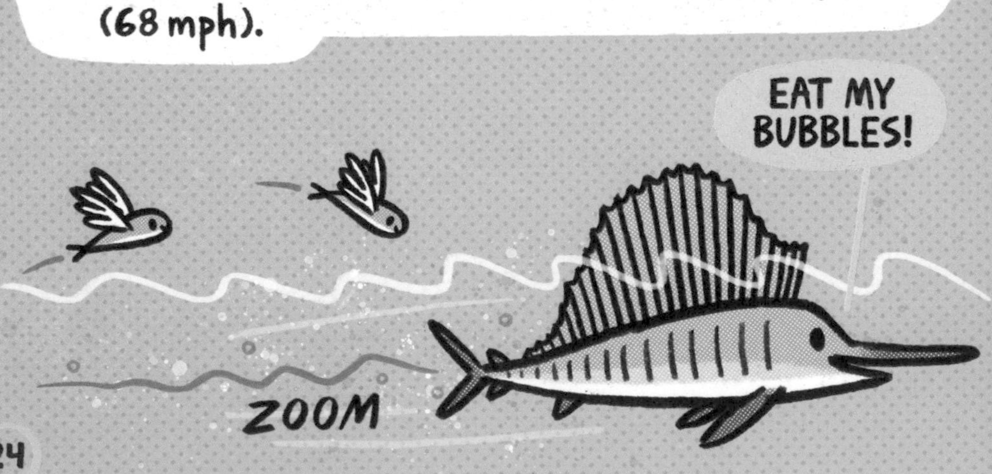
EAT MY BUBBLES!
ZOOM

NARWHAL, YOU'RE A

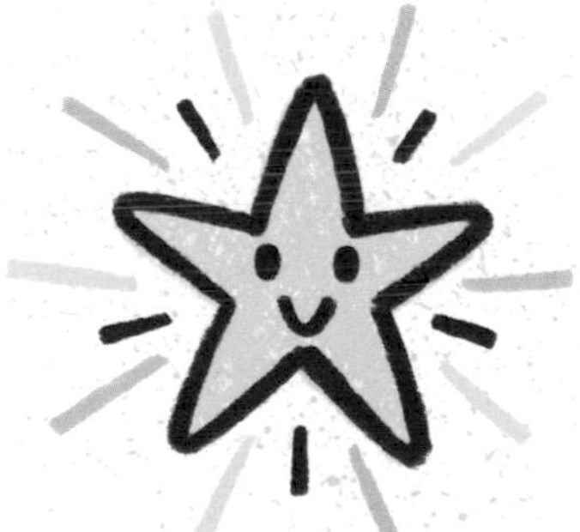

SUPERSTAR!

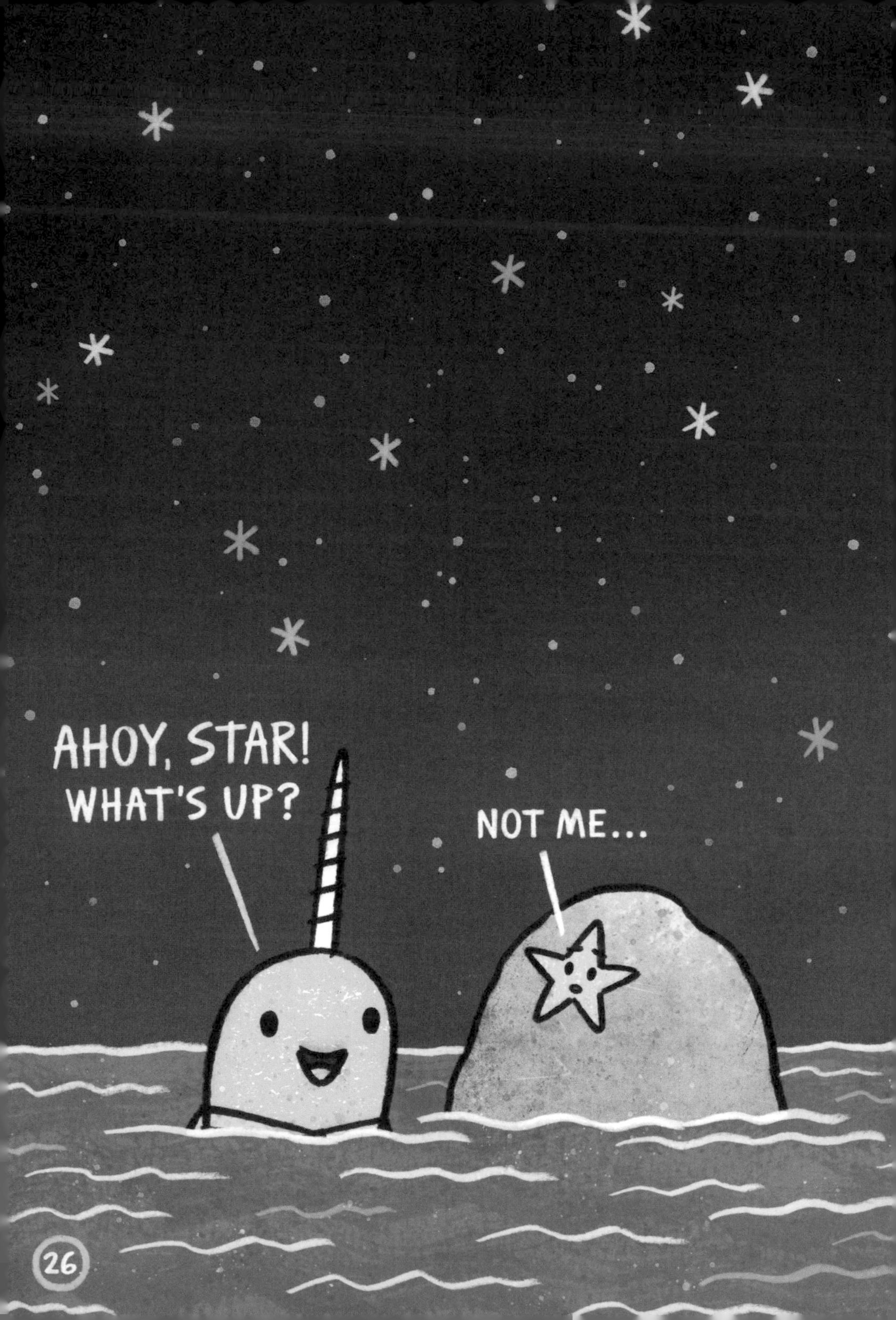
AHOY, STAR! WHAT'S UP?
NOT ME...

SOUNDS STELLAR!

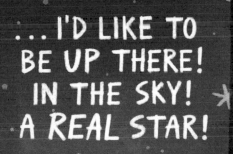

... I'D LIKE TO BE UP THERE! IN THE SKY! A REAL STAR!

MAYBE I AM A REAL STAR, BUT I FELL TO EARTH AND HIT MY HEAD OR SOMETHING AND NOW I DON'T REMEMBER!

MAYBE! WANT ME TO TRY THROWING YOU UP THERE?

OKAY!

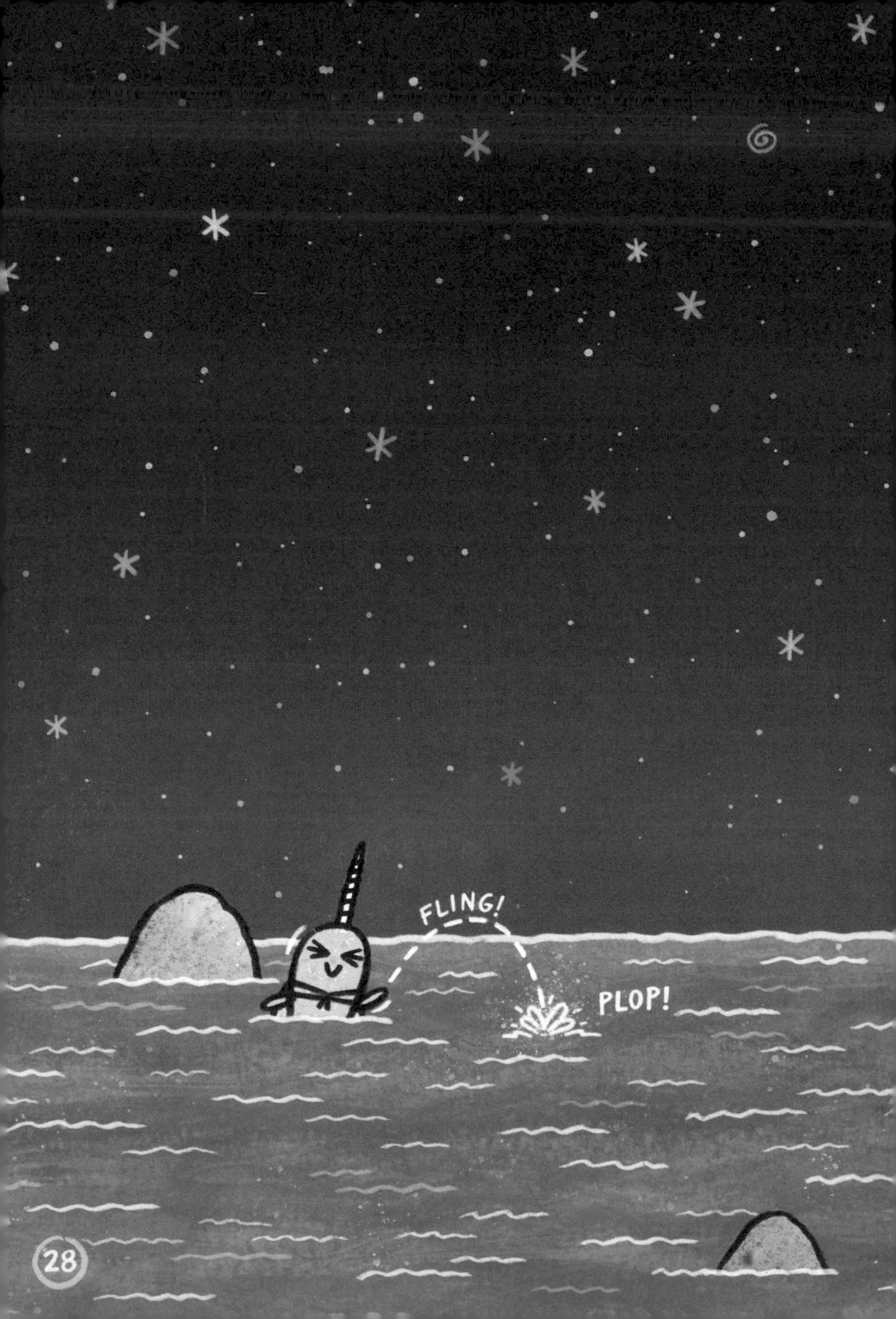
FLING!
PLOP!

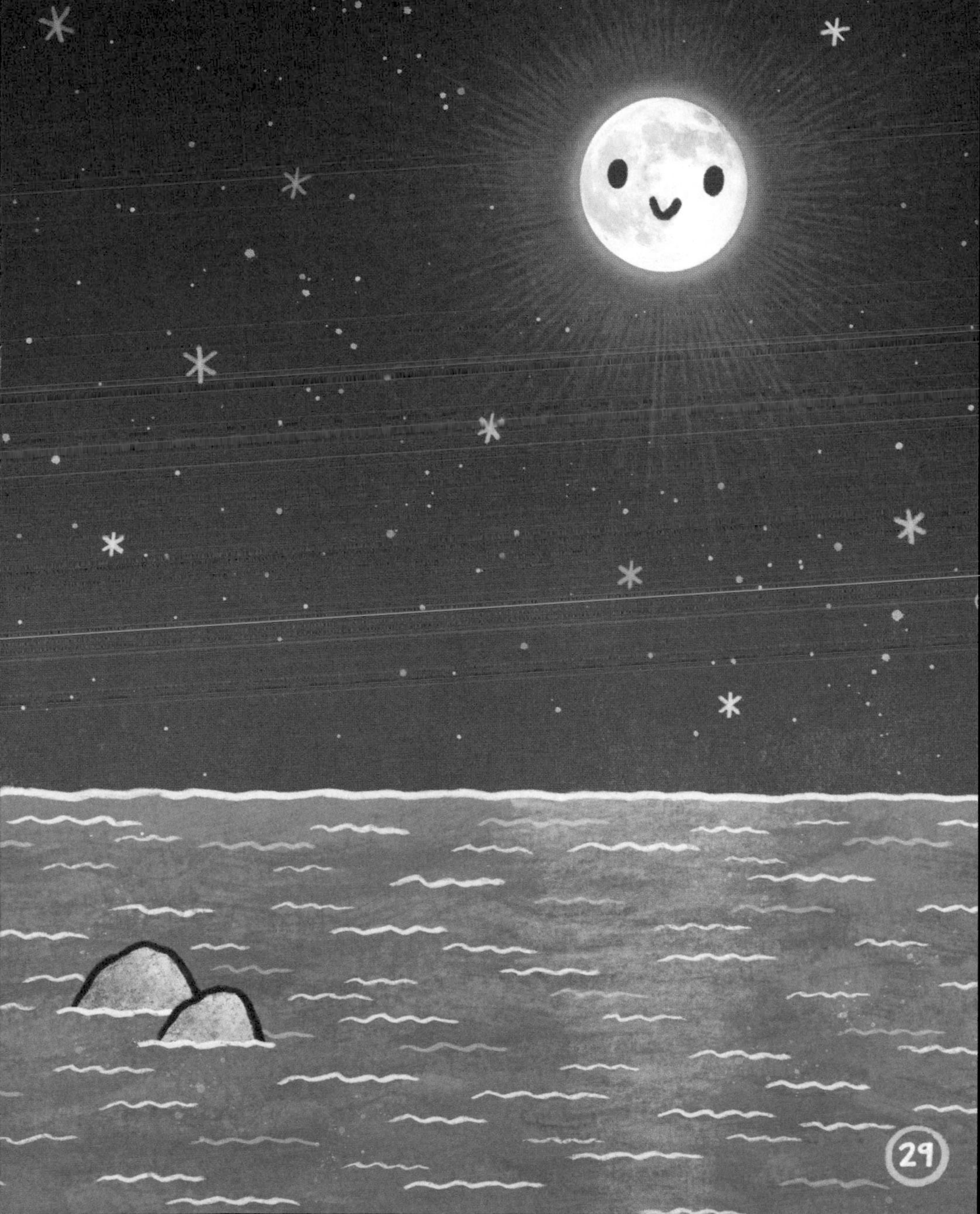

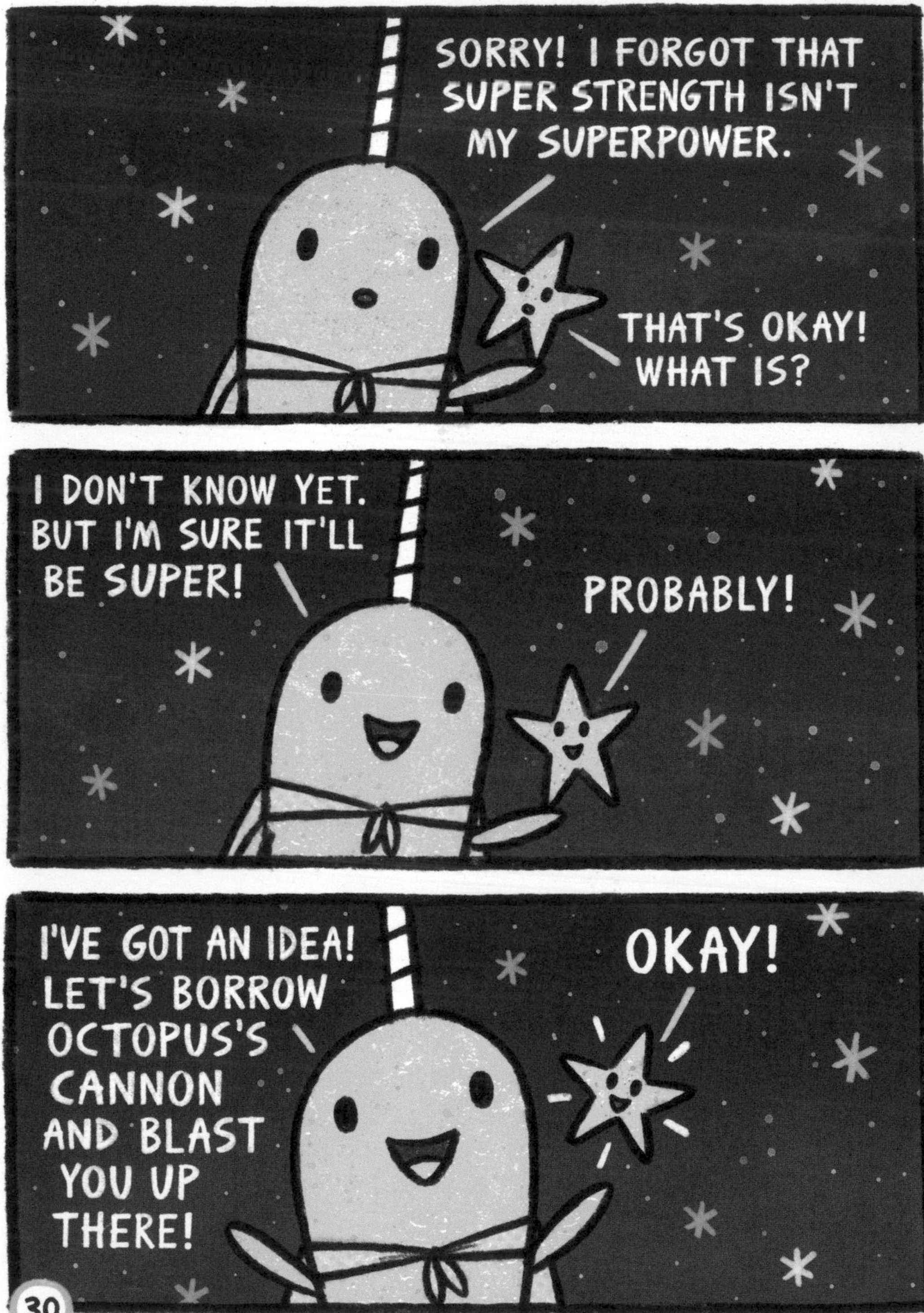
SORRY! I FORGOT THAT SUPER STRENGTH ISN'T MY SUPERPOWER.
THAT'S OKAY! WHAT IS?
I DON'T KNOW YET. BUT I'M SURE IT'LL BE SUPER!
PROBABLY!
I'VE GOT AN IDEA! LET'S BORROW OCTOPUS'S CANNON AND BLAST YOU UP THERE!
OKAY!

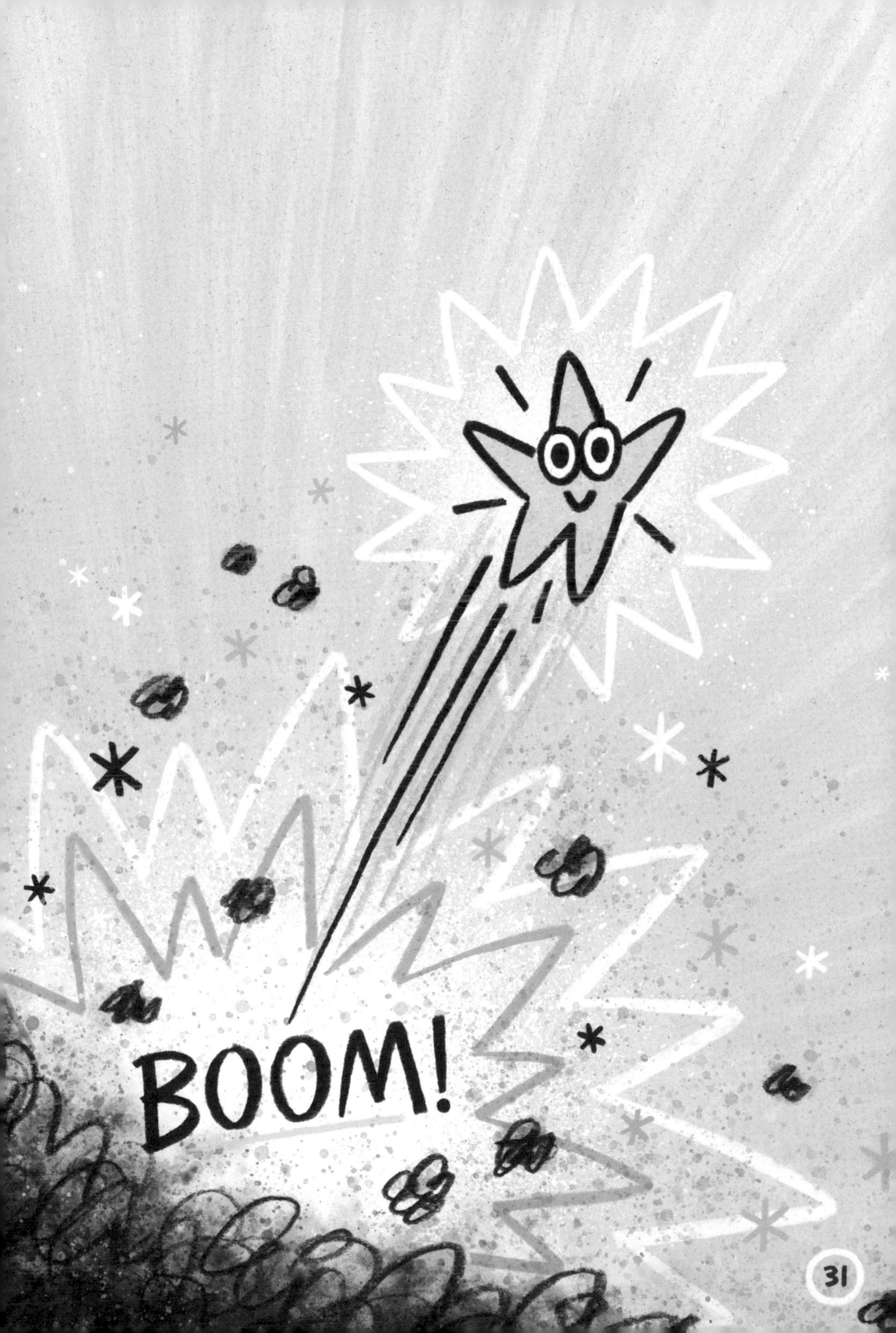
BOOM!

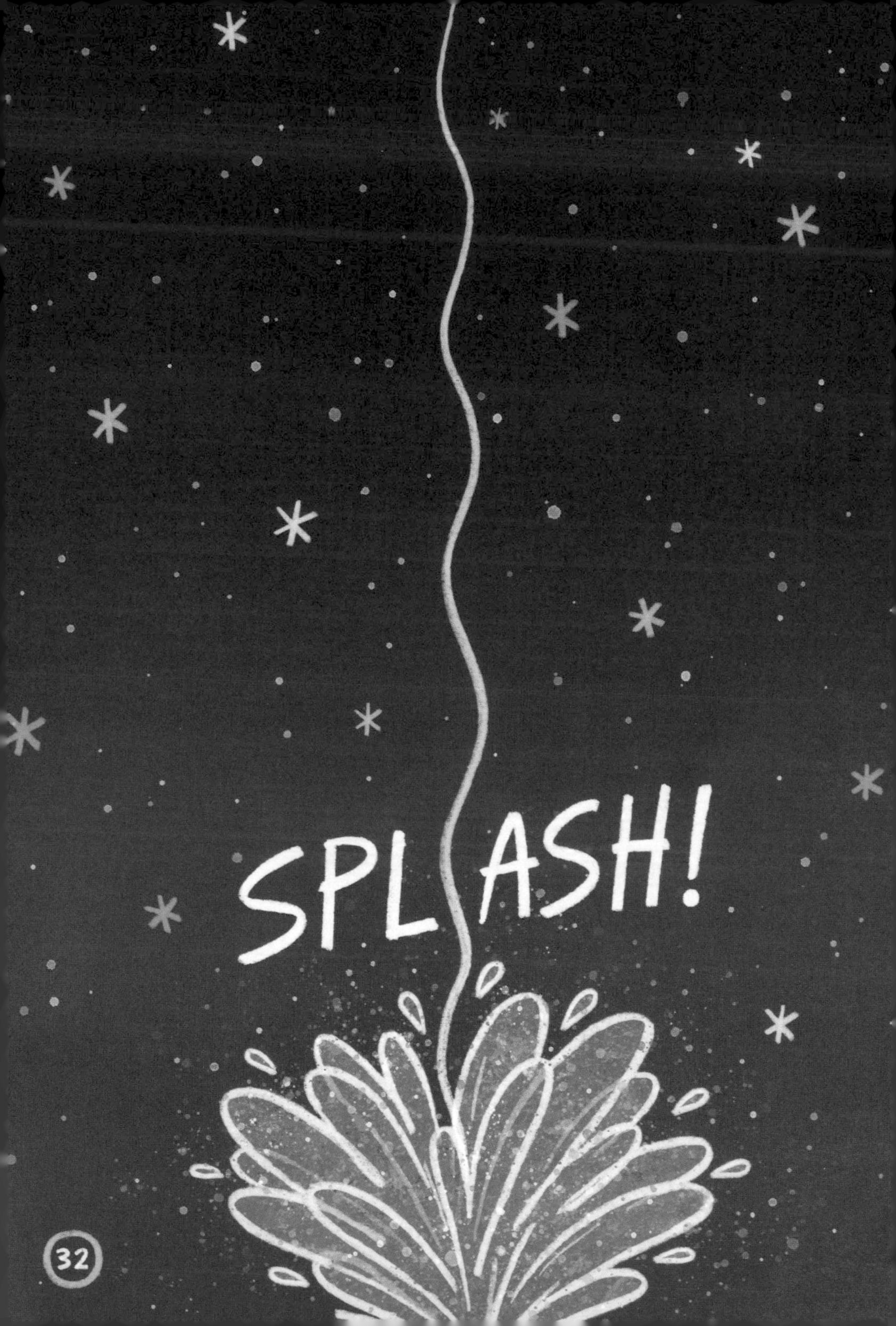
SPLASH!

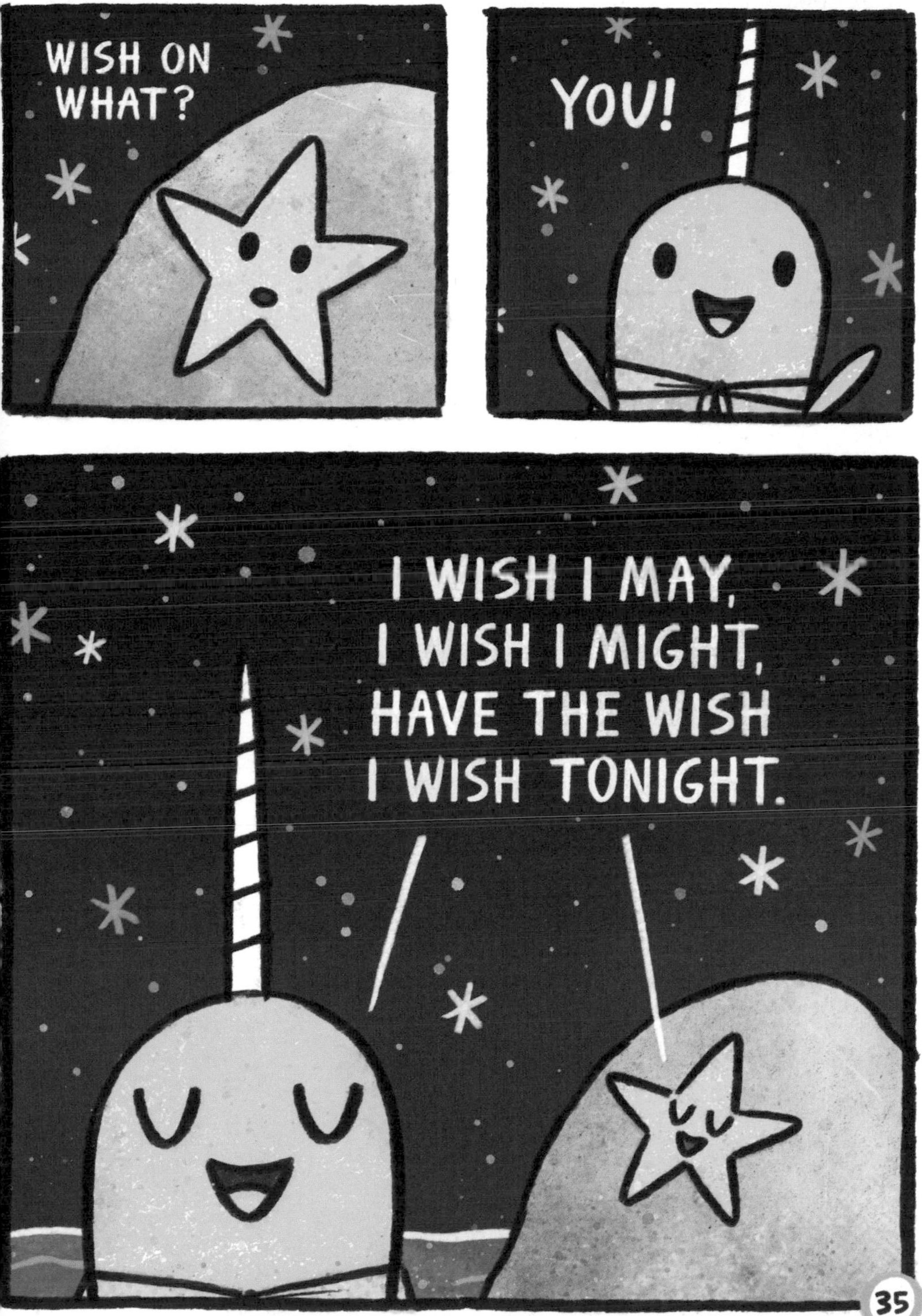
WISH ON WHAT?
YOU!
I WISH I MAY, I WISH I MIGHT, HAVE THE WISH I WISH TONIGHT.

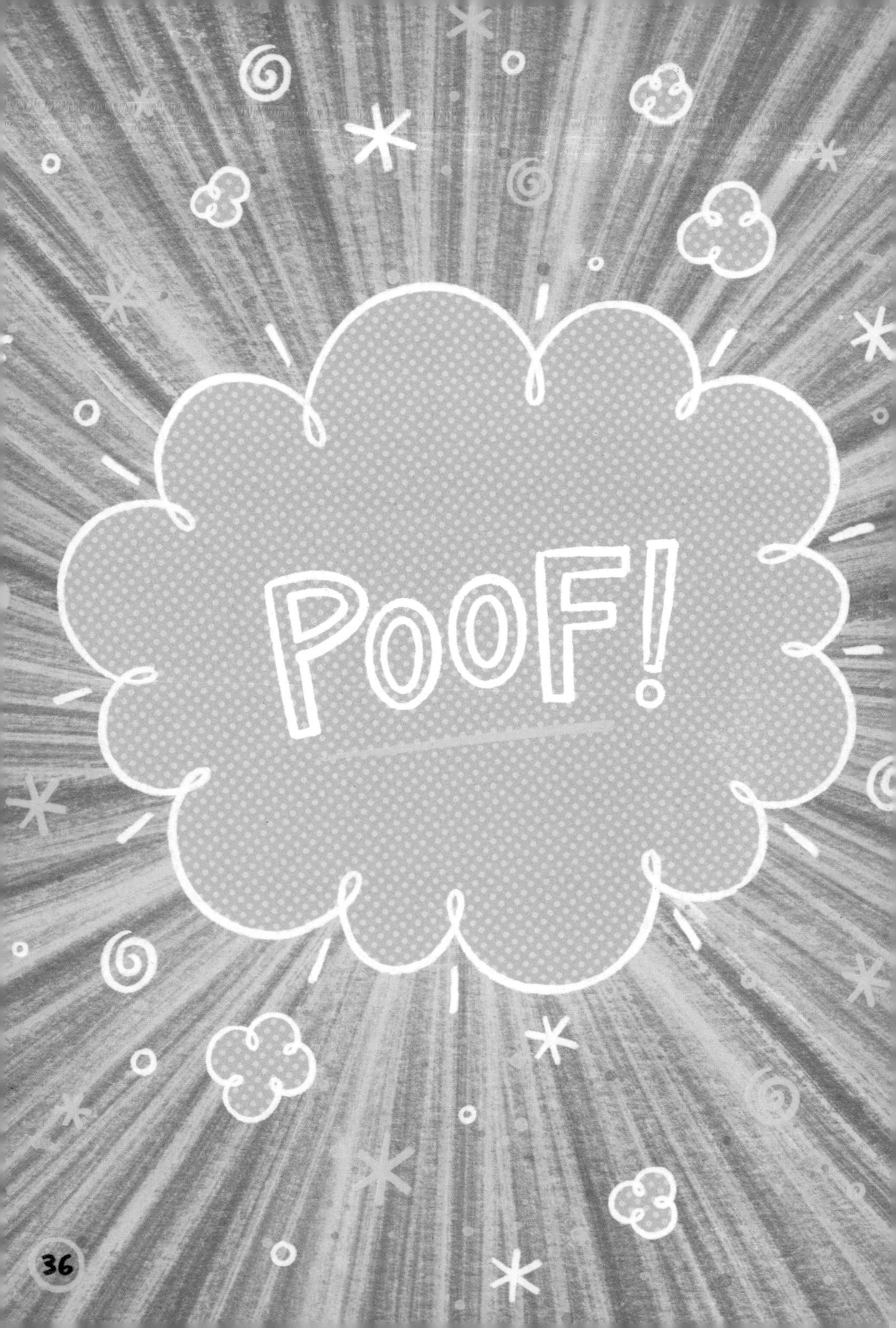
POOF!

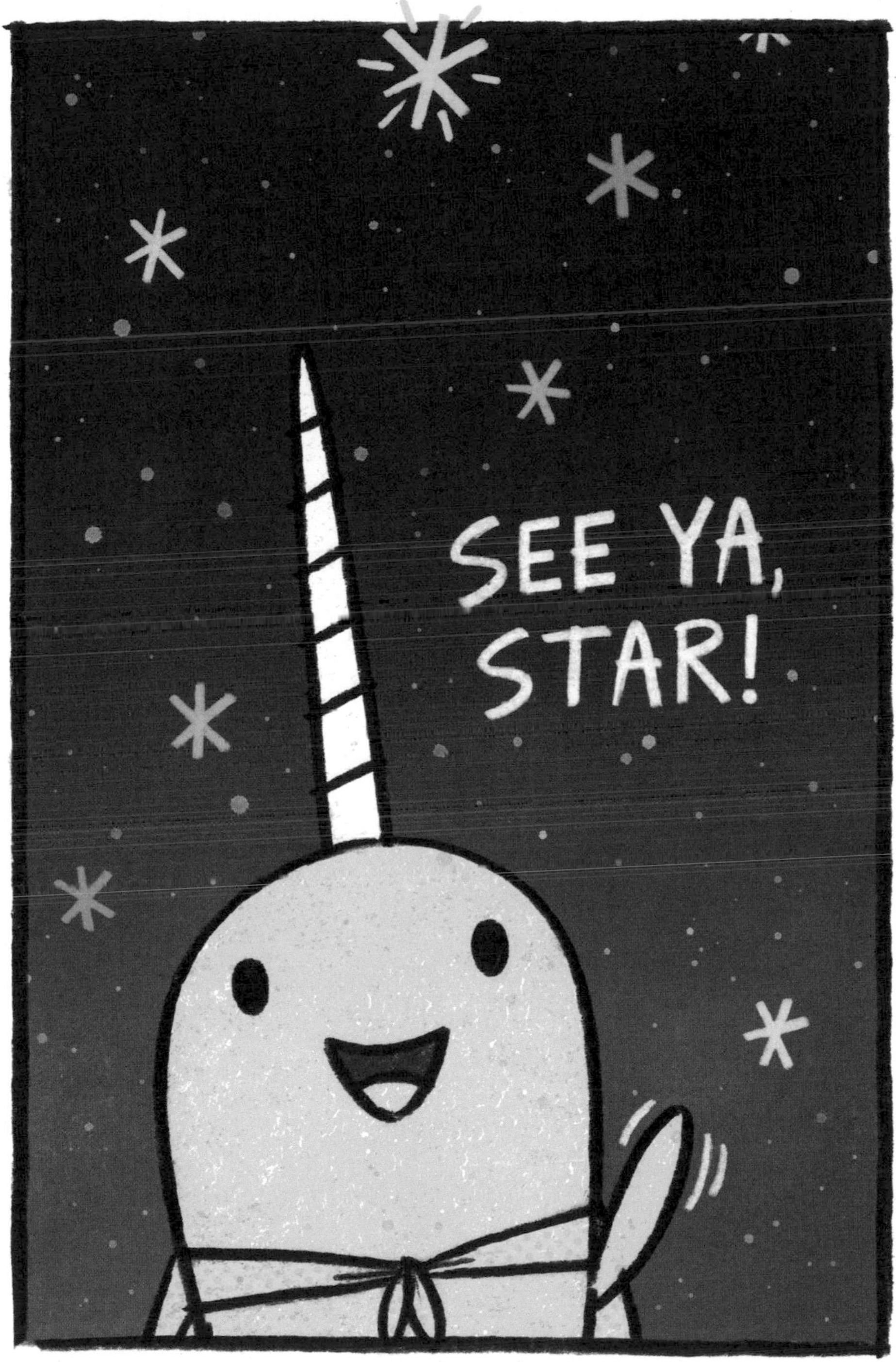
SEE YA, STAR!

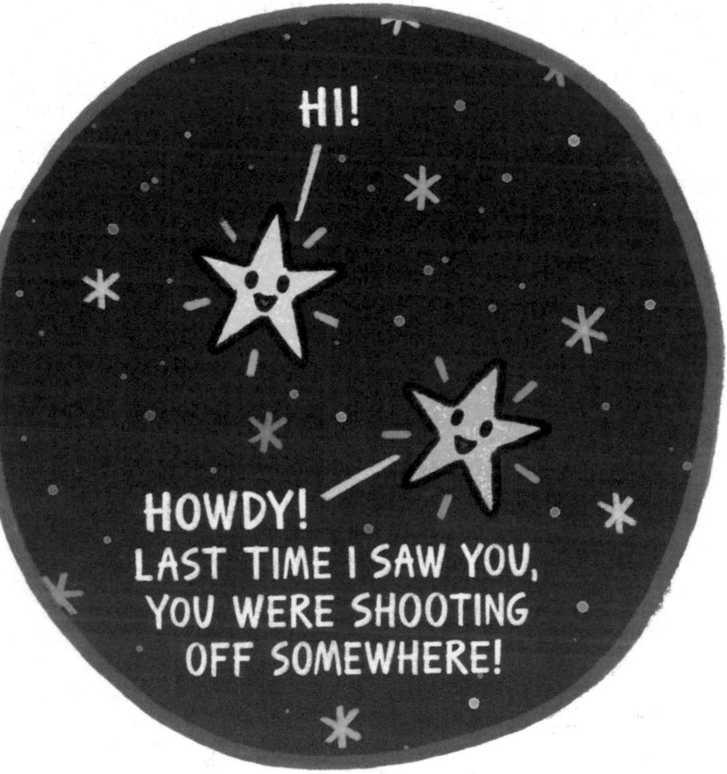
HI!
HOWDY!
LAST TIME I SAW YOU, YOU WERE SHOOTING OFF SOMEWHERE!

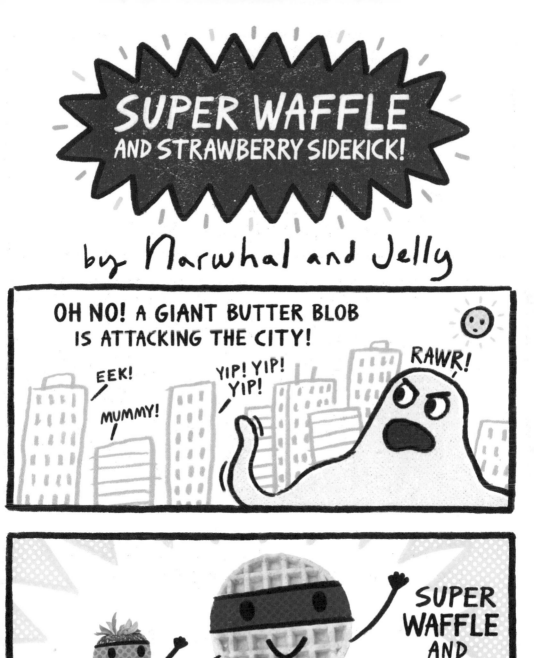

SUPER WAFFLE
AND STRAWBERRY SIDEKICK!

by Narwhal and Jelly

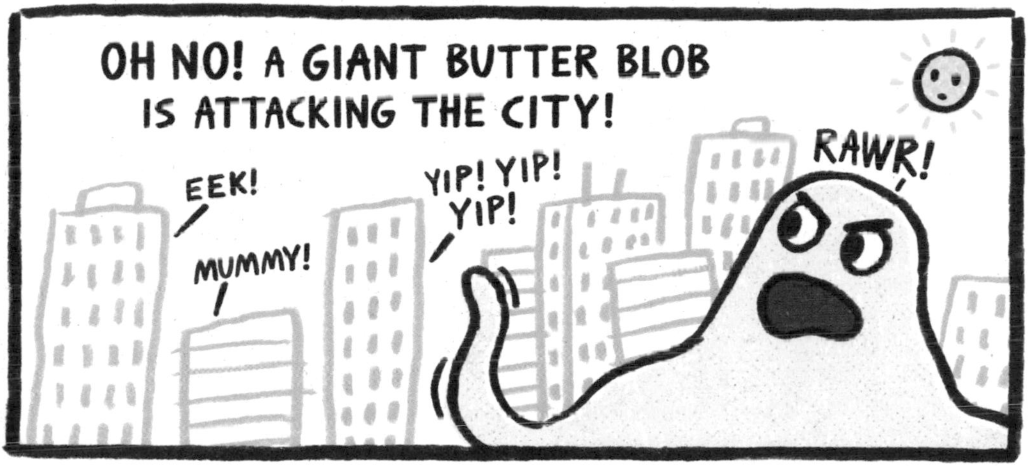
OH NO! A GIANT BUTTER BLOB IS ATTACKING THE CITY!
EEK!
MUMMY!
YIP! YIP! YIP!
RAWR!

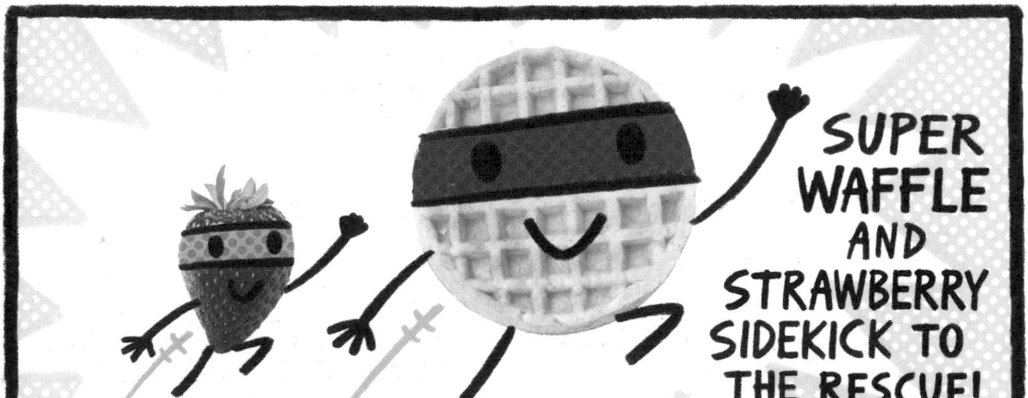
SUPER WAFFLE AND STRAWBERRY SIDEKICK TO THE RESCUE!

SUPER NARWHAL

VS

BLUE JELLY

A.K.A.

THE SUPER SUPERPOWER!

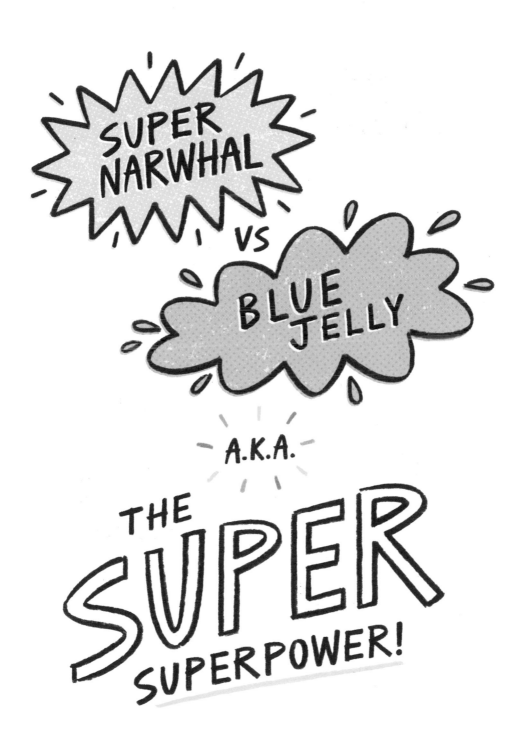

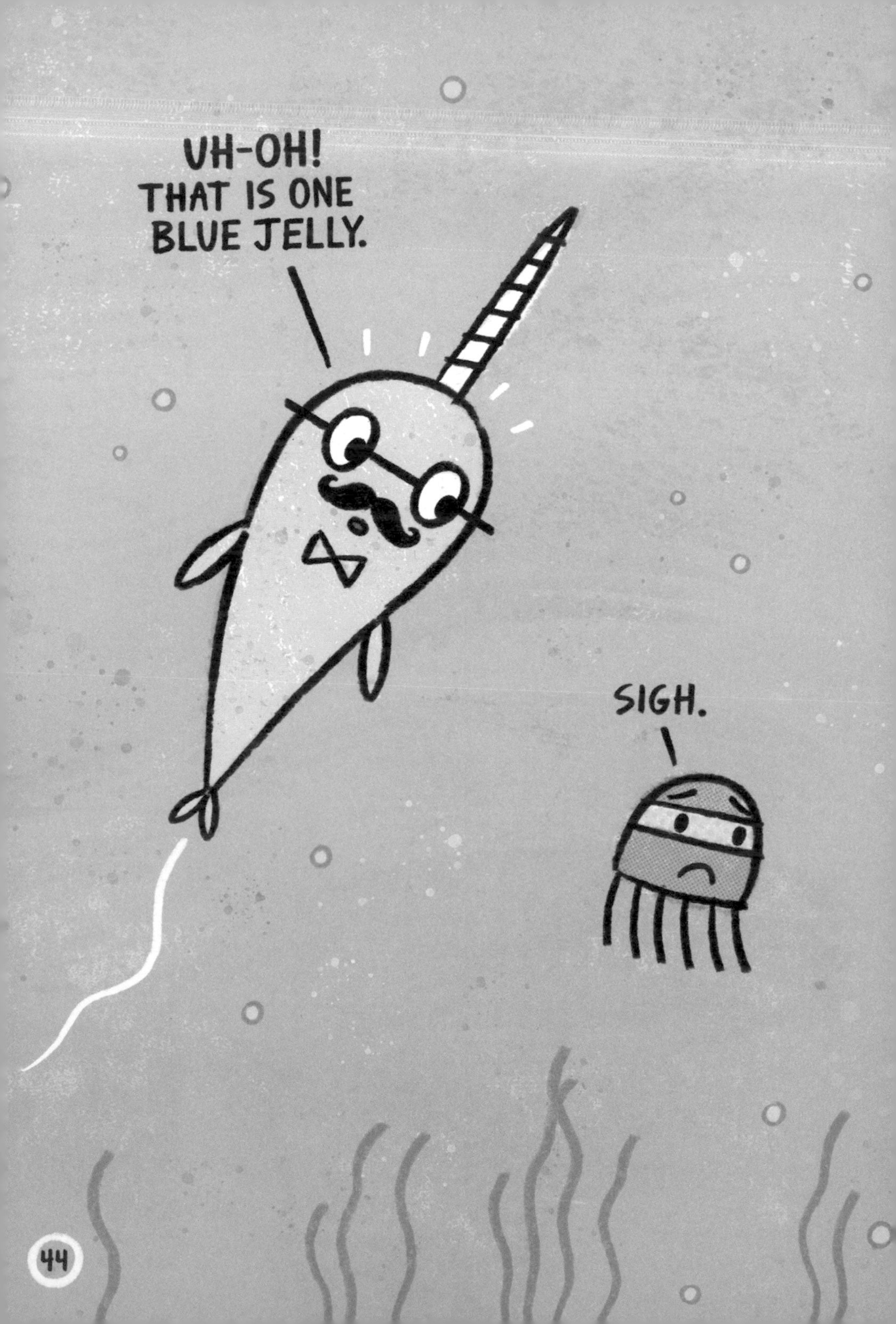
UH-OH!
THAT IS ONE
BLUE JELLY.
SIGH.

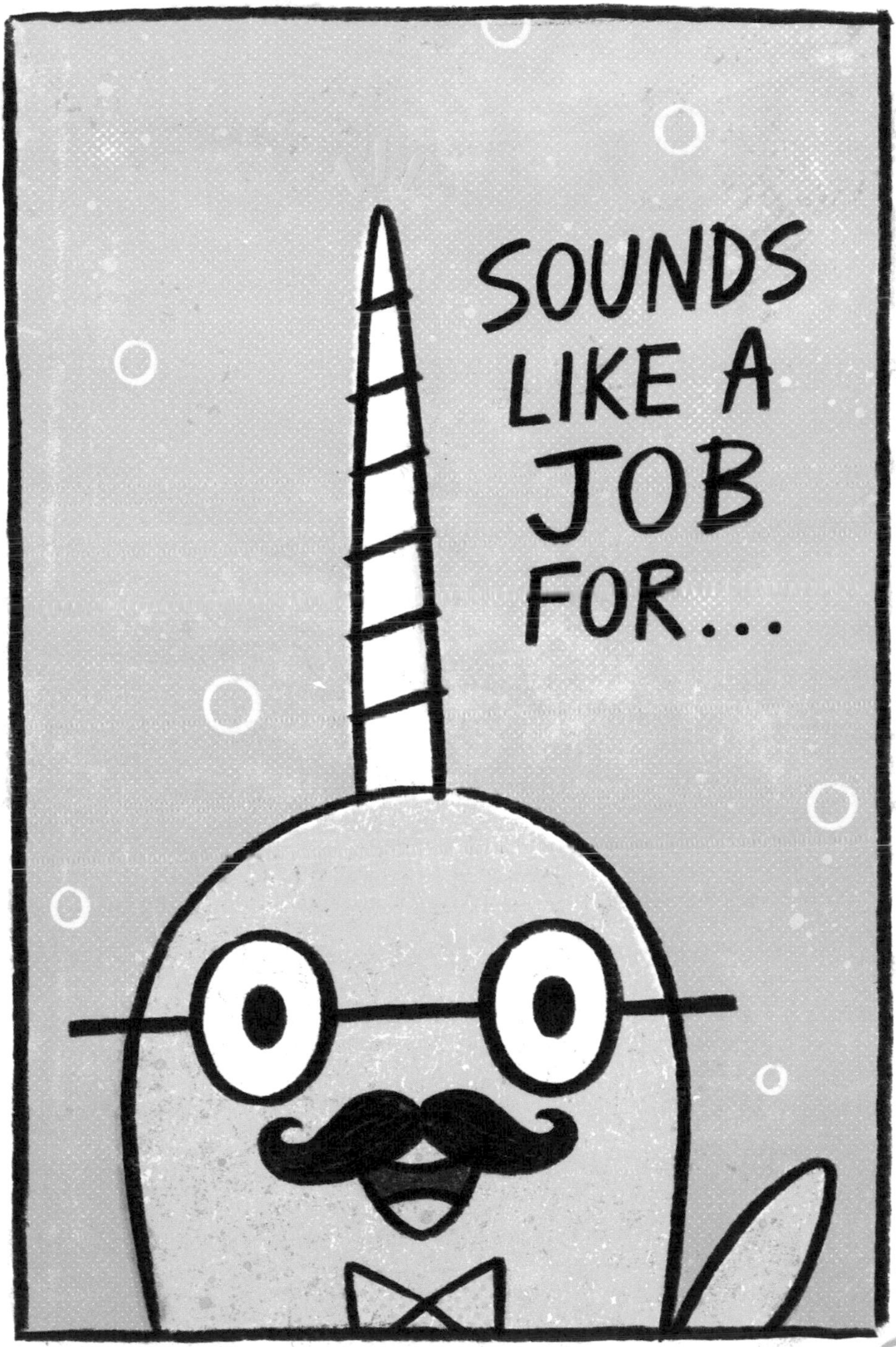
SOUNDS LIKE A JOB FOR...

SUPER NARWHAL!

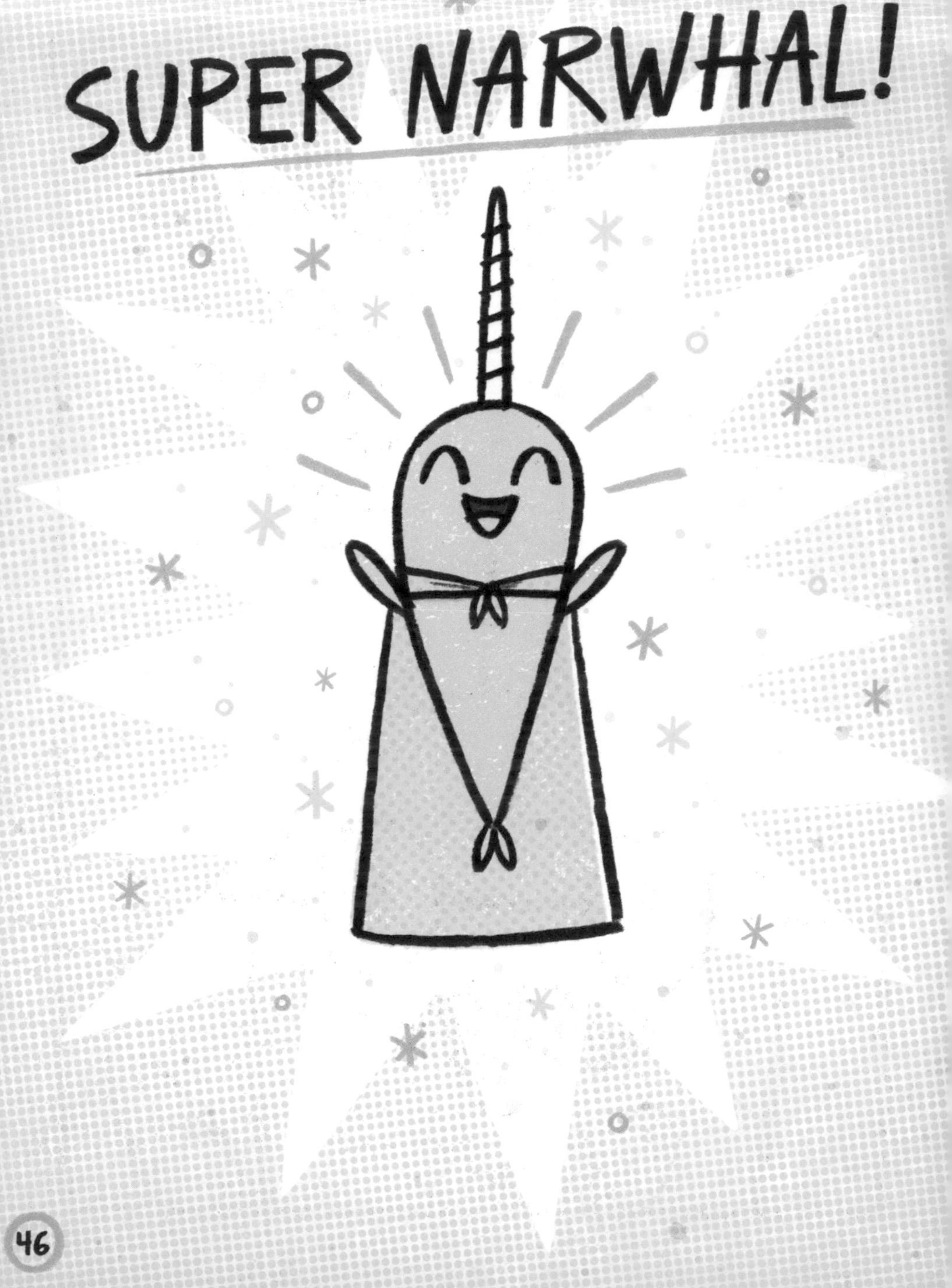

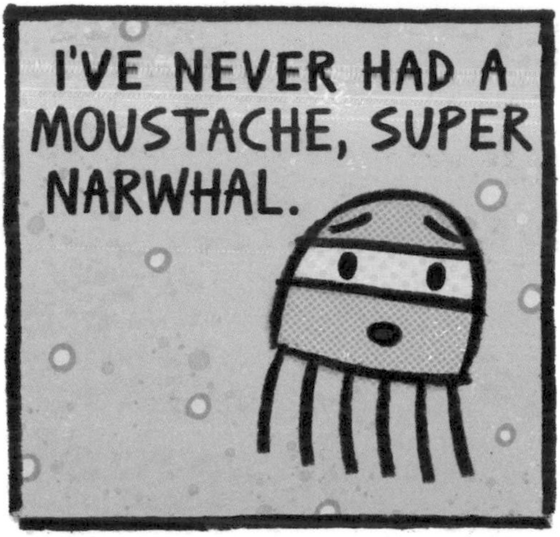
I'VE NEVER HAD A MOUSTACHE, SUPER NARWHAL.

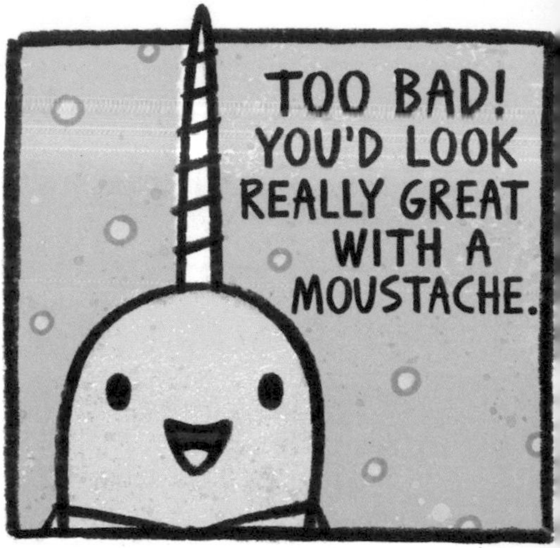
TOO BAD! YOU'D LOOK REALLY GREAT WITH A MOUSTACHE.

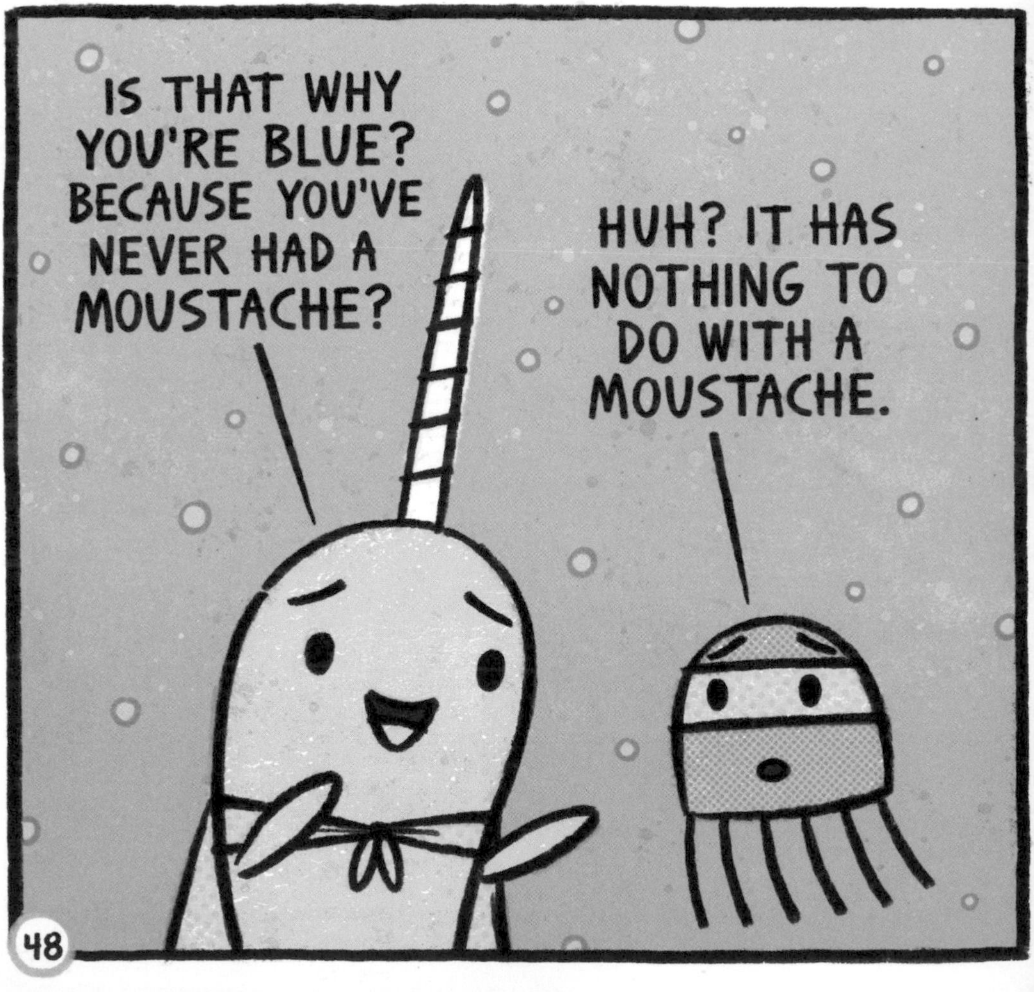
IS THAT WHY YOU'RE BLUE? BECAUSE YOU'VE NEVER HAD A MOUSTACHE?
HUH? IT HAS NOTHING TO DO WITH A MOUSTACHE.

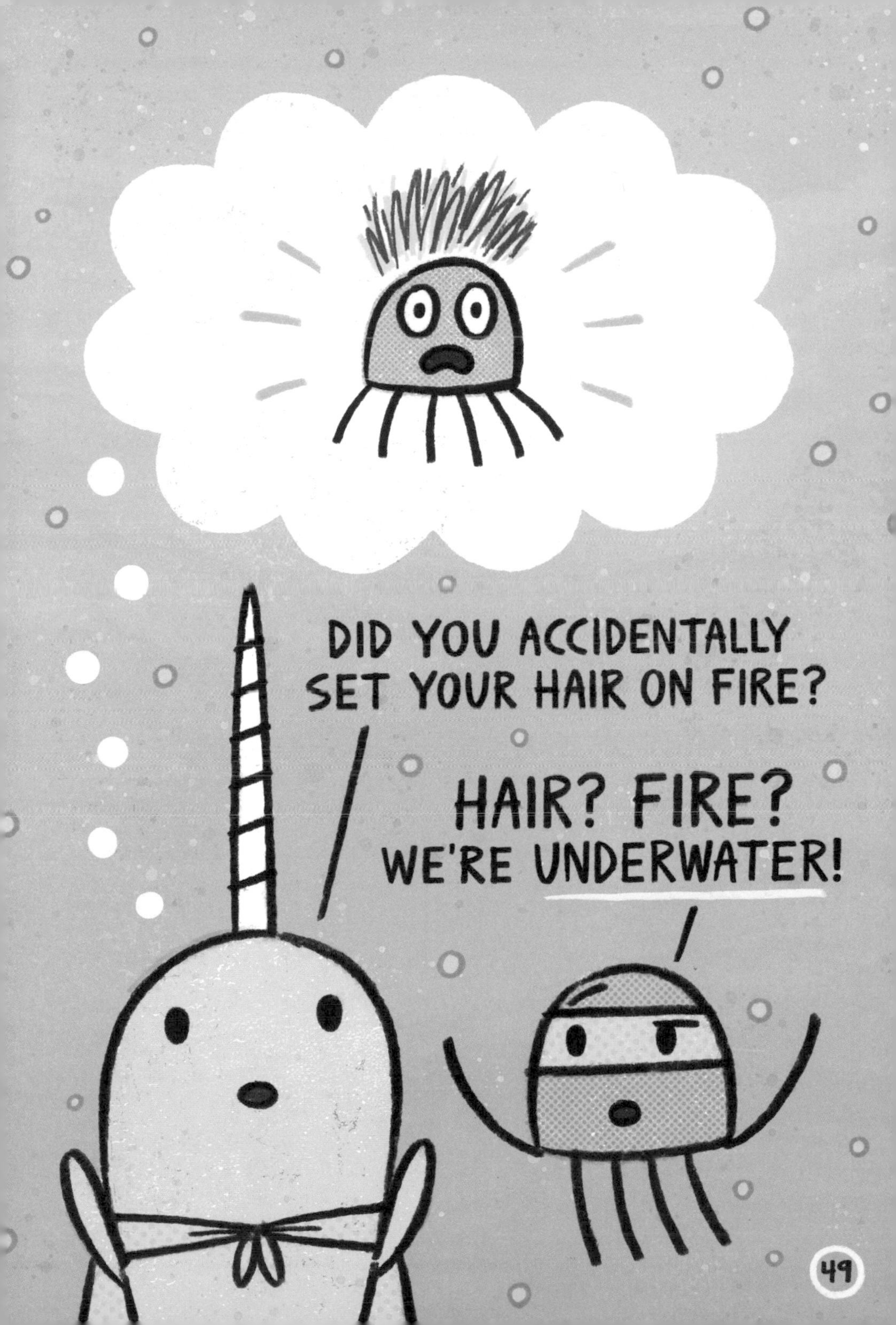
DID YOU ACCIDENTALLY SET YOUR HAIR ON FIRE?
HAIR? FIRE? WE'RE UNDERWATER!

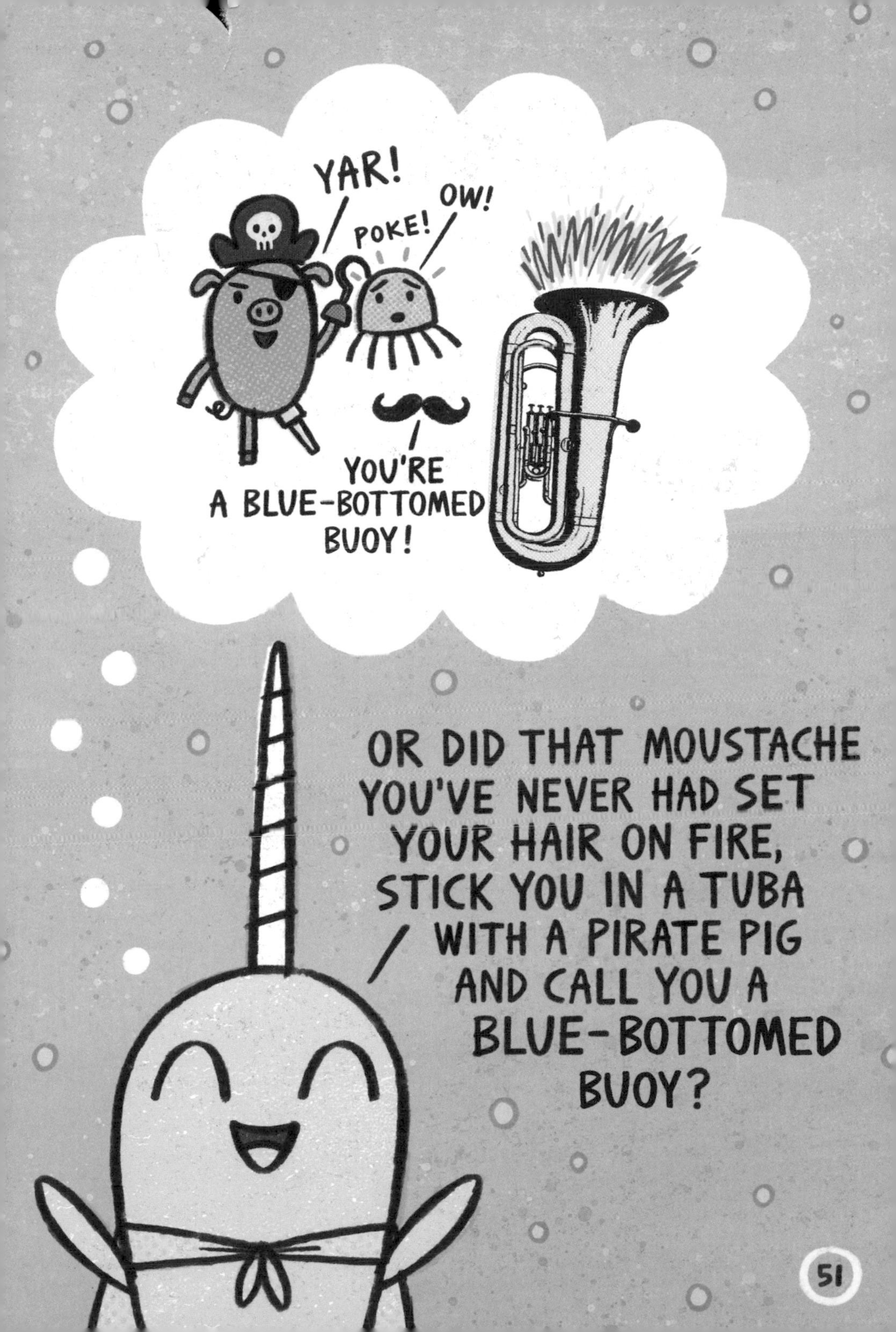
YAR!
POKE!
OW!
YOU'RE A BLUE-BOTTOMED BUOY!
OR DID THAT MOUSTACHE YOU'VE NEVER HAD SET YOUR HAIR ON FIRE, STICK YOU IN A TUBA WITH A PIRATE PIG AND CALL YOU A BLUE-BOTTOMED BUOY?

OH, WAIT, NOW I REMEMBER...

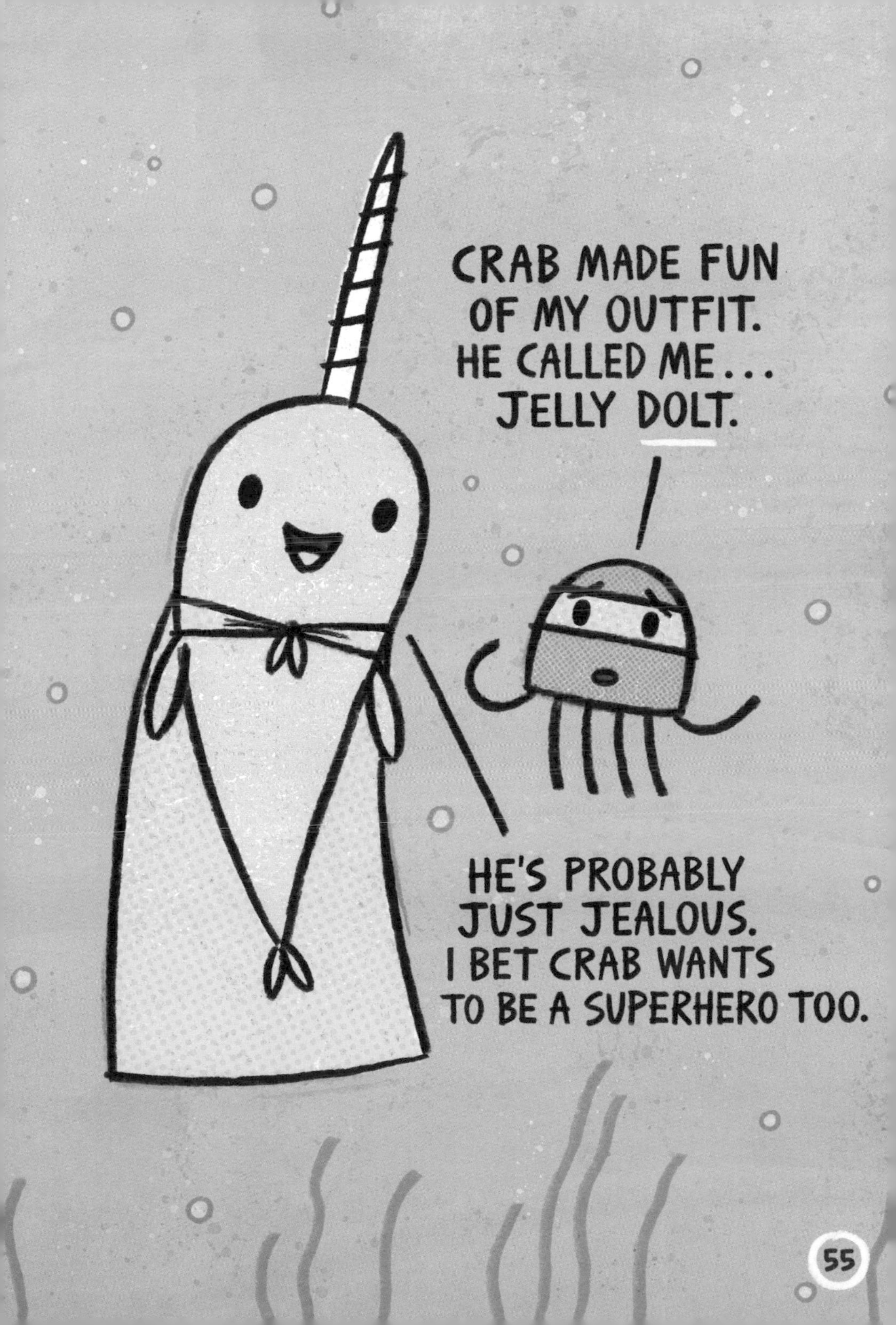
CRAB MADE FUN OF MY OUTFIT. HE CALLED ME... JELLY DOLT.
HE'S PROBABLY JUST JEALOUS. I BET CRAB WANTS TO BE A SUPERHERO TOO.

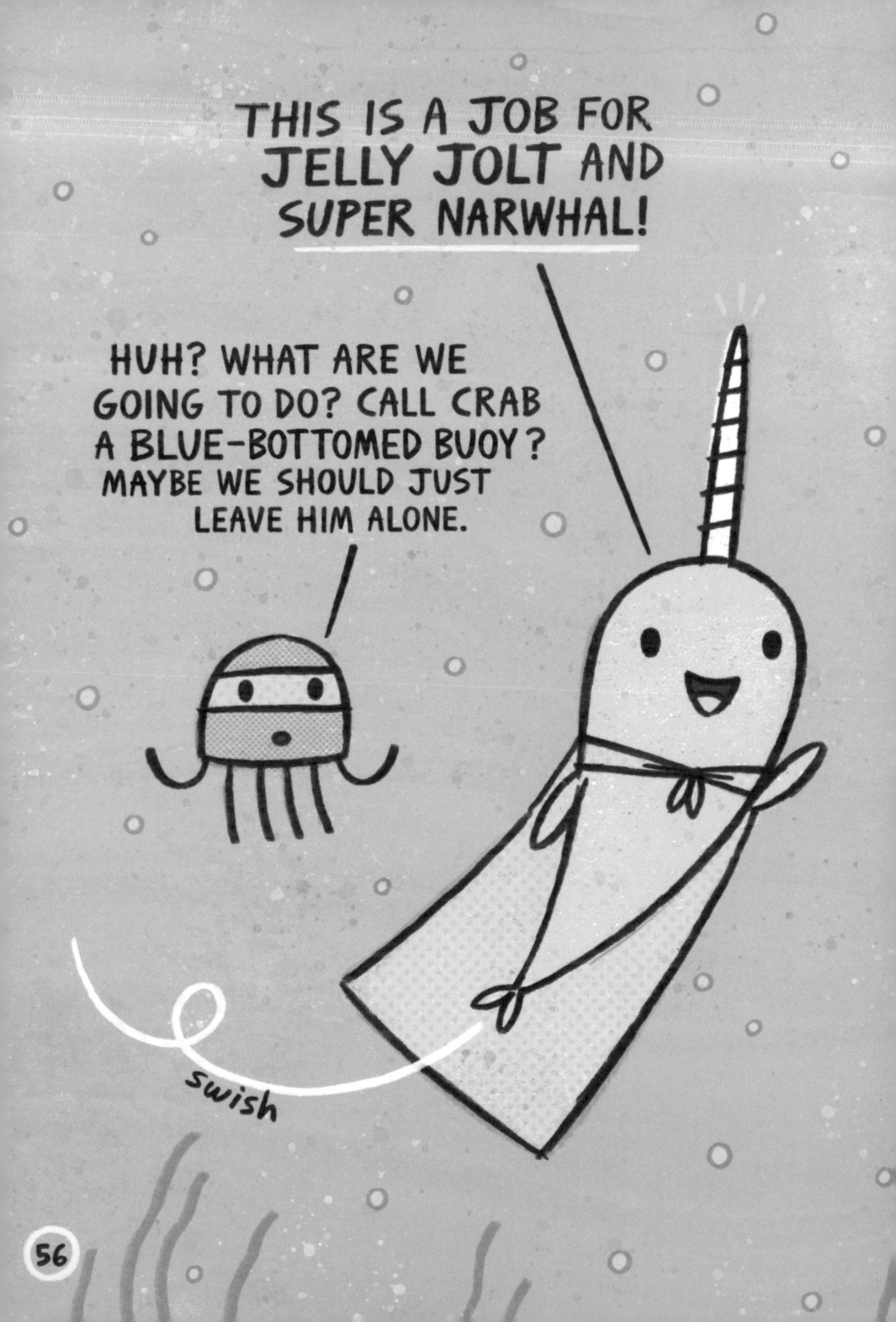
THIS IS A JOB FOR JELLY JOLT AND SUPER NARWHAL!
HUH? WHAT ARE WE GOING TO DO? CALL CRAB A BLUE-BOTTOMED BUOY? MAYBE WE SHOULD JUST LEAVE HIM ALONE.
swish

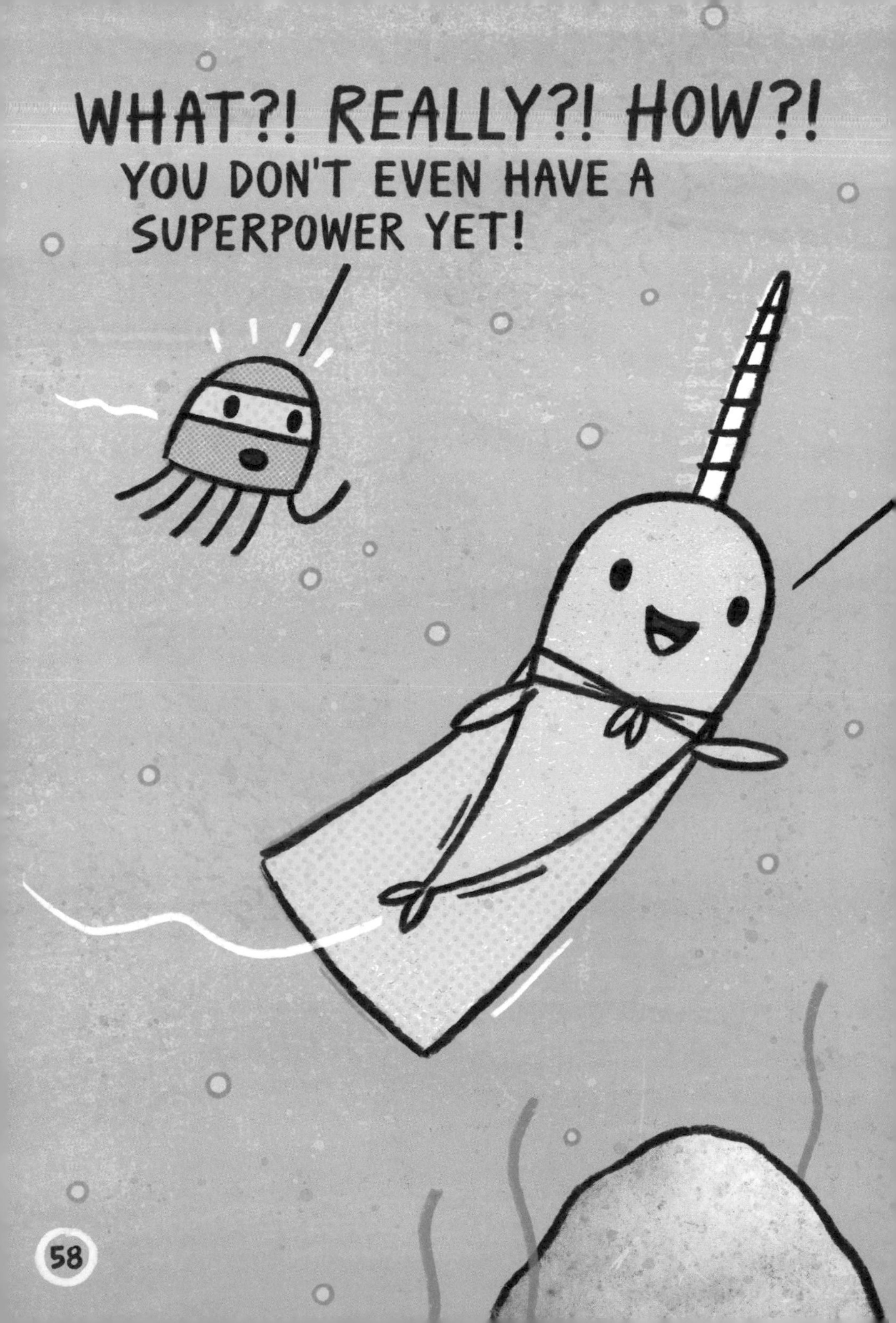
WHAT?! REALLY?! HOW?!
YOU DON'T EVEN HAVE A SUPERPOWER YET!

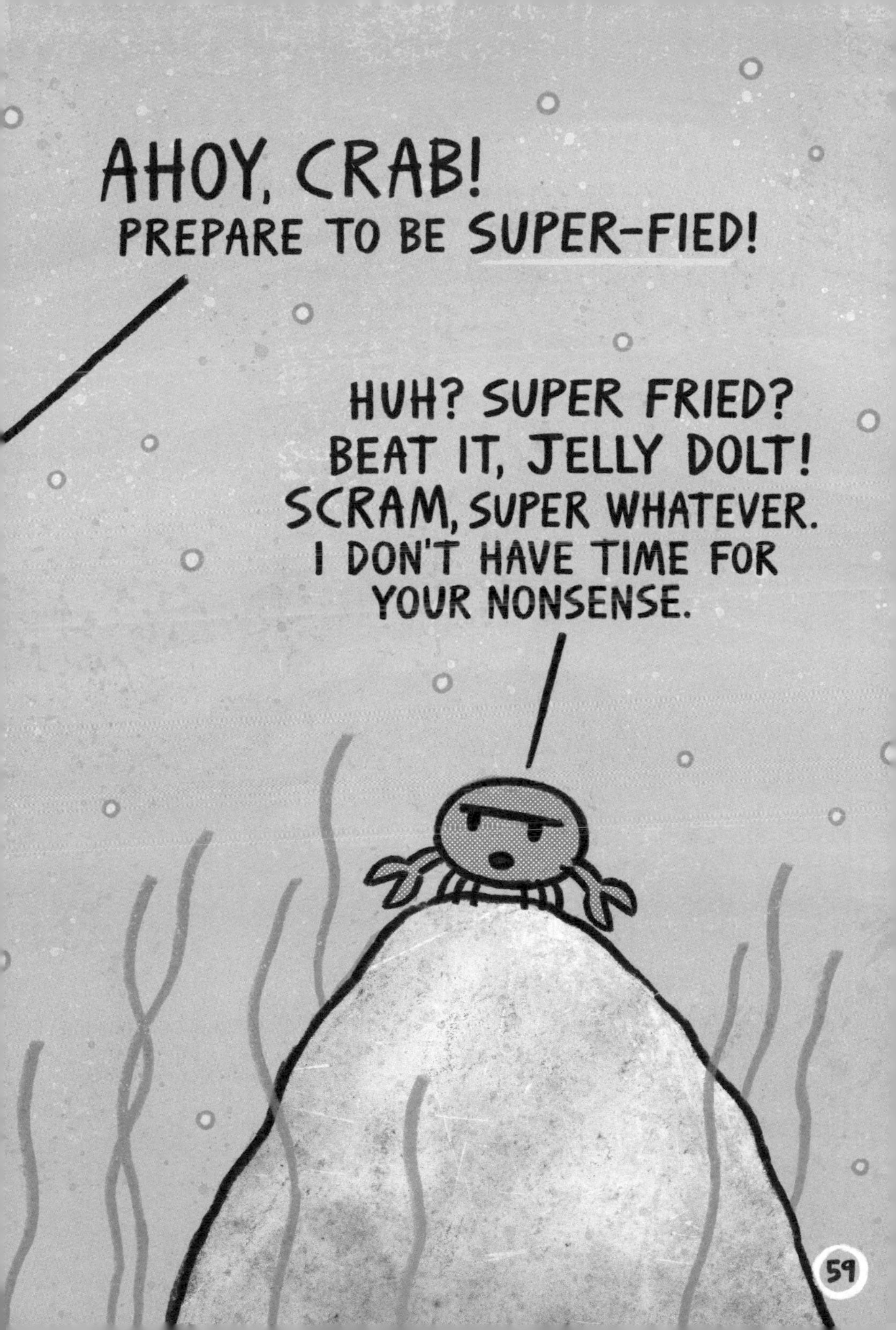
AHOY, CRAB!
PREPARE TO BE SUPER-FIED!
HUH? SUPER FRIED? BEAT IT, JELLY DOLT! SCRAM, SUPER WHATEVER. I DON'T HAVE TIME FOR YOUR NONSENSE.

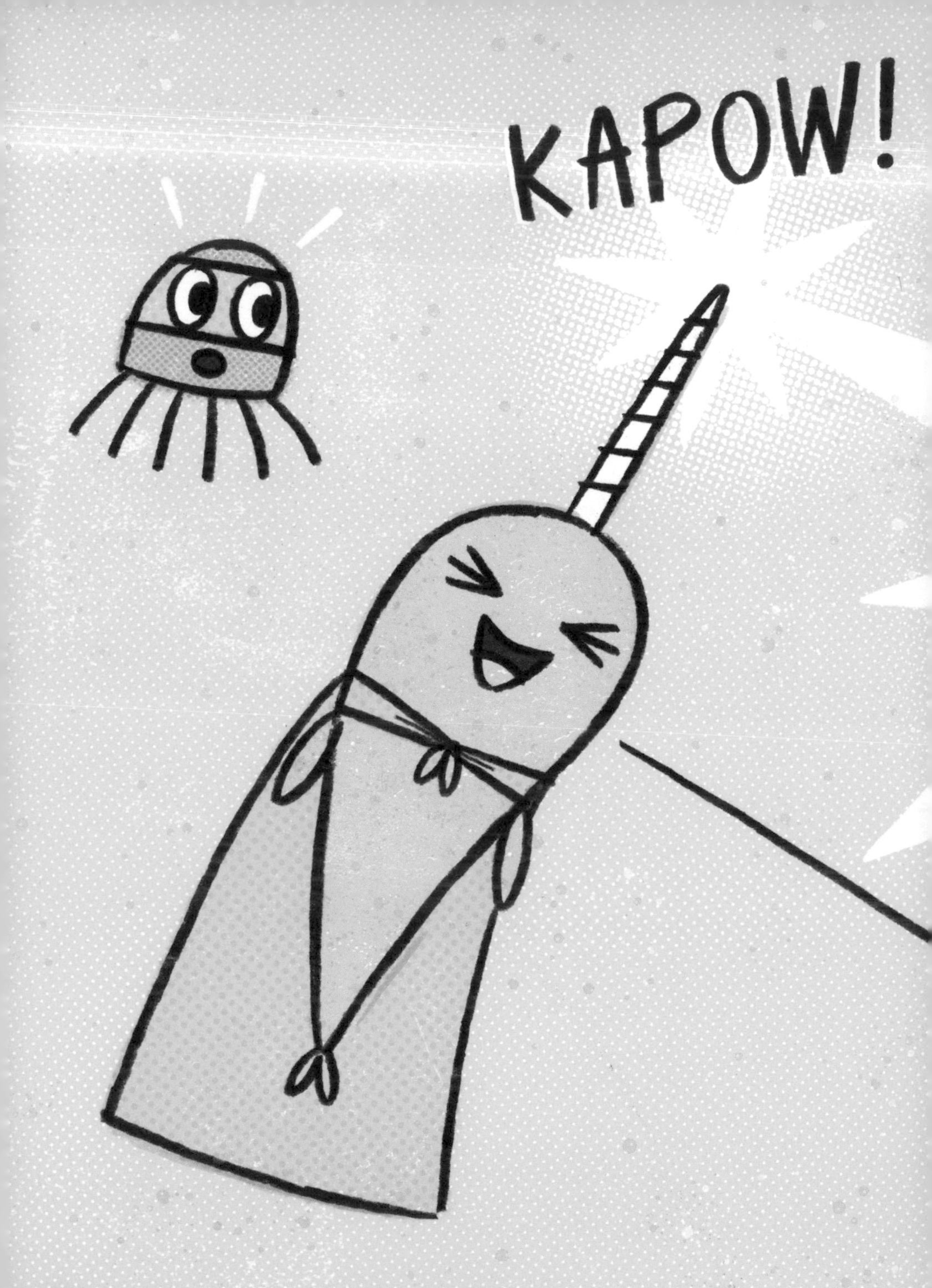
KAPOW!

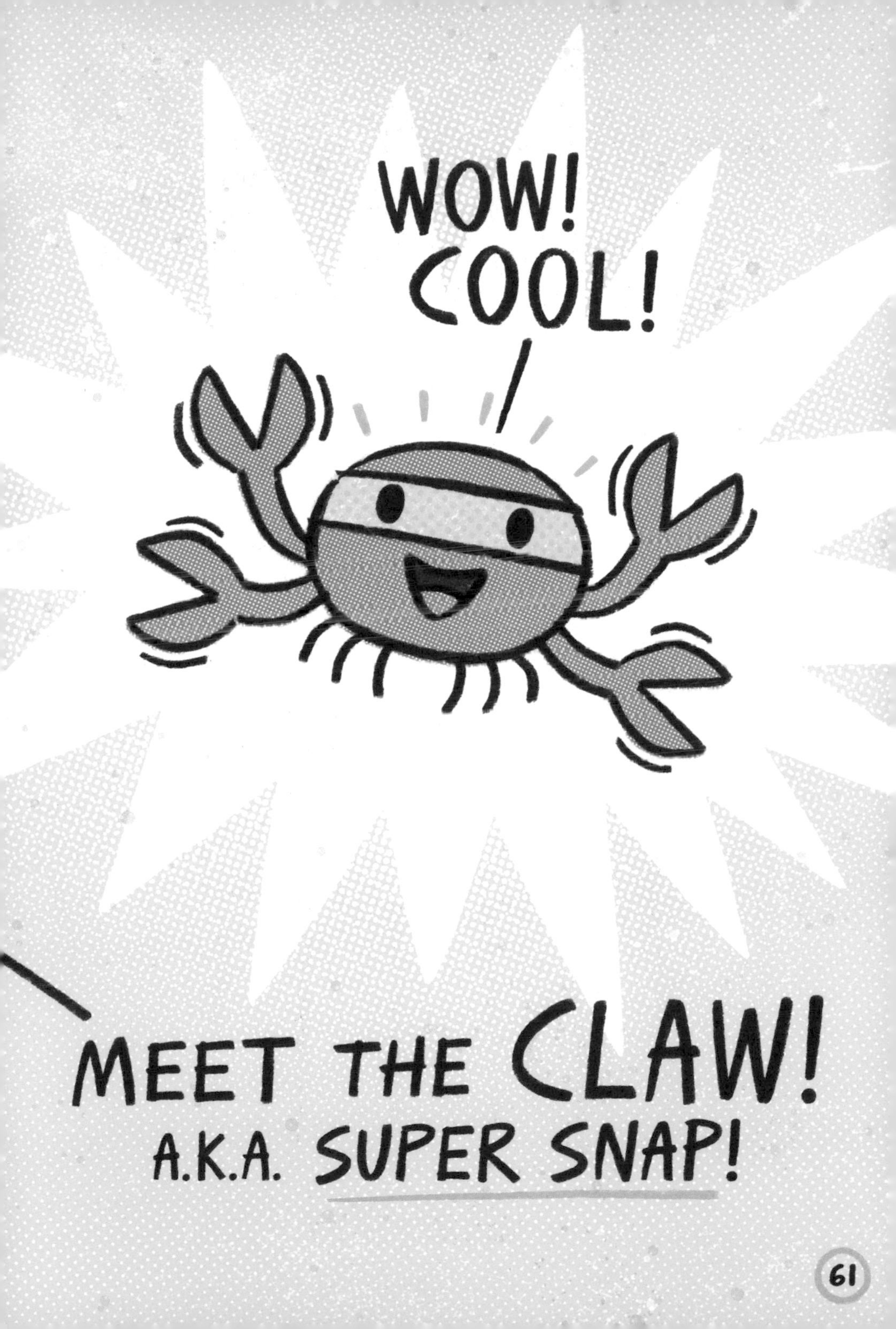
WOW! COOL!
MEET THE CLAW!
A.K.A. SUPER SNAP!

WHOA! I CAN'T BELIEVE IT! YOUR SUPERPOWER IS THE POWER TO BRING OUT THE SUPER IN OTHERS!

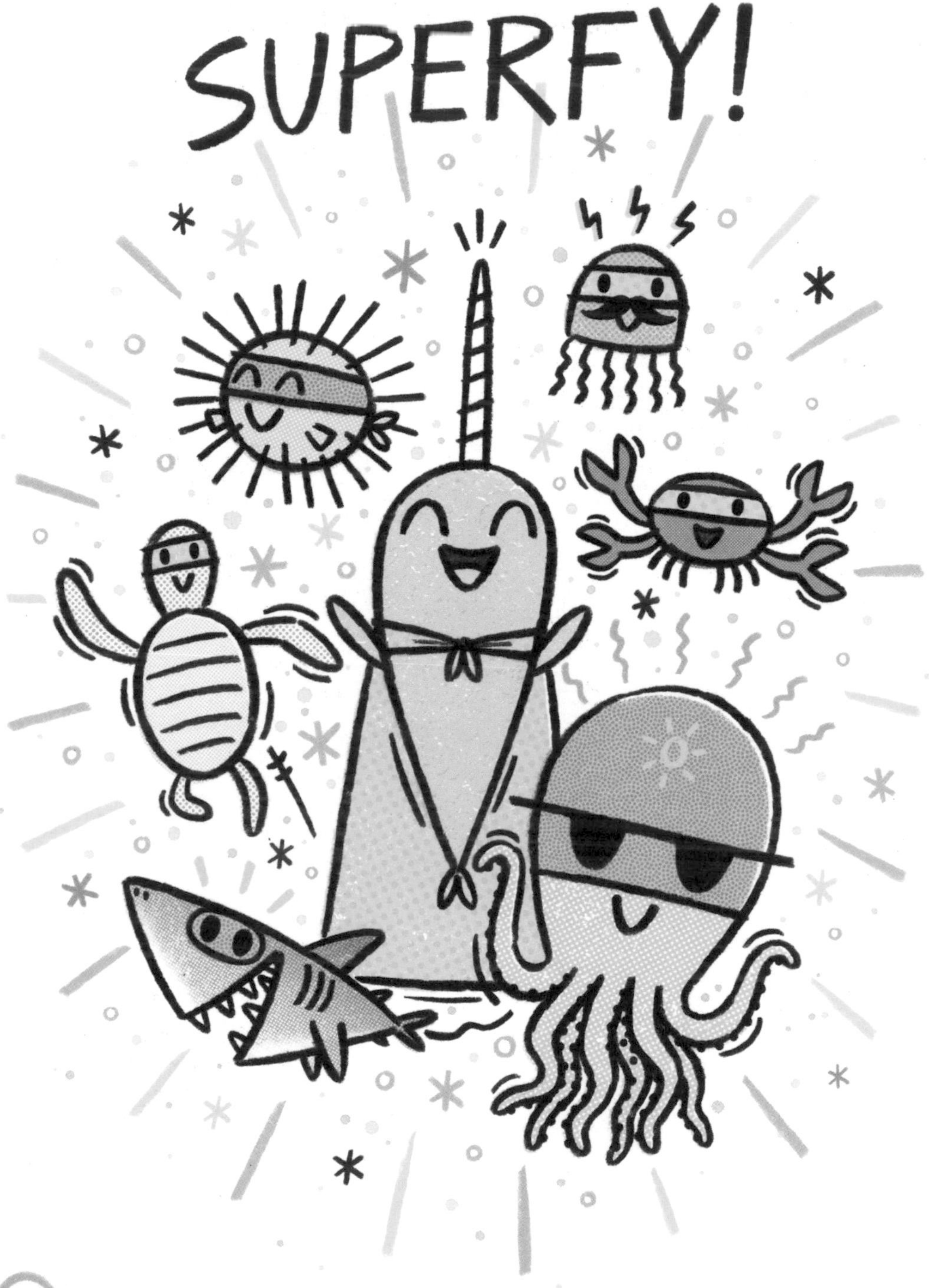
SUPERFY!